recoil

recoil

jim thompson

VINTAGE CRIME / **BLACK LIZARD**

vintage books • a division of random house, inc. • new york

First Vintage Crime/Black Lizard Edition, January 1992

Library of Congress Cataloging-in-Publication Data
Thompson, Jim, 1906–1977.
Recoil/by Jim Thompson. — 1st Vintage Crime/Black Lizard ed.
p. cm. —(Vintage Crime/Black Lizard)
ISBN 0-679-73308-6
I. Title. II. Series.
[PS3539.H6733R4 1992]
813'.54—dc20   91-50629   CIP

Manufactured in the United States of America
10 9 8 7 6 5 4 3 2 1

recoil

doc luther 1

Quietly he tested the door of Lila's bedroom and saw that it was locked; and then he went into his own room, leaving the door open to hear any movement of hers, and opened his briefcase.

He took the insurance policies from the briefcase, scanned them perfunctorily and slipped them into his inside coat pocket. They would go into the safety deposit box tomorrow.

He dipped into the briefcase again and drew out other papers. He studied them, frowning, with much of the disturbing feeling that he had for the insurance policies. With a grunt of irritation, he shuffled them into a kind of chronological order and began to read:

SANDSTONE STATE REFORMATORY

Luther Psychological Clinic
Capital & Lee Sts.
Capital City

Gentlemen:
This is a rather unusual application for em-

ployment. I hope you will read it to the end, and give it your earnest consideration.

I am thirty-three years old, a high school graduate, and, through reading and study, possess the equivalent of at least two years of college. I weigh one hundred and seventy pounds and am five feet eleven inches tall. Despite serious handicaps, I have kept myself in good physical condition. I am not familiar with your business, and do not know what type of job you might have at your disposal. But I will welcome the chance for any kind of work—within the state—and at whatever wage you care to pay.

For the past fifteen years I have been an inmate of this institution, serving a sentence of ten years to life for bank robbery. The crime was not one to be taken lightly, and I have not. But, in all humility, I cannot see that any good purpose is served in detaining me here longer.

I became eligible for parole approximately five years ago. Unfortunately, my parents had died and my only other relative, a married sister, was not and is not in a position to act in my behalf. I was, of course, too young to have formed business associations at the time of my commitment. As you doubtless know, a prospective parolee must have a job before he can be released; he must establish his ability to support himself. I am asking that you help me to do this.

May I please hear from you? On second thought, will you simply take action on my case with the parole board in the normal way of an interested party for an inmate? You can find out anything you wish to know about me from the board, and

this will obviate any misunderstanding that might arise here from my writing you.
Very truly yours,
Patrick M. Cosgrove (No. 11587)
Librarian, Sandstone State Reformatory

Sandstone ...
Luther thought he'd become accustomed to rottenness. Yet Sandstone never failed to outrage him. It wasn't a prison. It was a madhouse in which the keeper, and not the inmates, was mad. There was only one way to survive there: to become tougher and more tortuous-minded than that keeper. If you did that—if you amused the man with the preternaturally brilliant eyes and the unpredictable laughter—you not only survived, but did so in comparative comfort.
But there could be no letting down. You might tire of the game, but the man never did. And when you tired or became careless ...

SANDSTONE STATE REFORMATORY
Office of the Warden

Dr. Roland Luther
Capital & Lee Sts.
Capital City
        In re, Pat "Airplane Red" Cosgrove

Dear Doc:
Sure was good to hear from you and wish I was right there in the big town with you. I always say you was one perfect host and know how to entertain a man and that was sure some time the last time me and you and them other

fellows got together. Well, I was pretty hot when I got your letter and I was going to go right in and give that sob something to think about. But since you ask otherwise why that's the way it is and hands off, and anyway I could not help laughing when I got to thinking about it. You know the Chief, my secretary. Well I know Chief got that letter and probly a hundred others out for him but just try and make them say so. I bet we could hang them both and they wouldn't. I am a great admirer of loyalty and mind your business and know you are too. So you fix things up anyway you want but let me know how and I will play with you as far as I can. Just give me a ring when you are coming. I will close now as I am writing this myself instead of that sob chief and we will give them both a hell of a surprise.

> Yr. obdt. frnd. & servt.,
> Yancey Fish

P.S. Doc you know it is against the rules to bring whiskey into the prison and if I find a case or two on you I will have to confiskate it. Ha ha. Y.F.

Well, Fish hadn't hanged them, but he had threatened them with everything else; and, while each had faced the harangue in his own way, the results had been identical.

The Chief, a full-blooded Indian serving three life sentences, had merely grinned insolently and made non-committal replies. The red-haired, blue-eyed Cosgrove had talked at length: polite, mildly humorous, insistently grammatical—and without saying anything. He would not turn on the man, the Chief, who had obviously helped him. No threat or bribe could make him.

He, Luther, had been a little troubled by Cosgrove's patent intelligence. But still, he fitted specifications in every other detail, and he would be given nothing for that intelligence to work on.

OFFICE OF THE GOVERNOR

To Yancey L. Fish
Warden, Sandstone State Reformatory

GREETINGS:

Whereas it appears you now have in your keeping one Patrick M. Cosgrove, and

Whereas the said Patrick M. Cosgrove has served fifteen years of an indeterminate sentence and has met certain other conditions by which he becomes eligible for parole, and

Whereas one Roland T. Luther, Ph.D., a citizen in good standing, has guaranteed employment for the said Patrick M. Cosgrove during the two years succeeding the date of this instrument, pledging moreover that he will in every way assist the said Cosgrove to a righteous manner of living,

Therefore Let It Be Known that Patrick M. Cosgrove is hereby paroled in the custody of Roland T. Luther for a period of two years, or until and/or unless it should become necessary to remand the said Cosgrove to his present place of incarceration.

Let it further be known that upon satisfactory completion of the aforementioned term of parole, the said Patrick M. Cosgrove is to be restored to full citizenship and all rights and privileges accruing thereto.

WITNESS OUR HAND AND SEAL.
Louis Clements Clay
Governor, and President (pro tem)
Board of Parole

Well, there it was; the beginning and the end of everything. And now that he had examined it item by item, he could not dispel the thought that it was both foolish and dangerous. If Hardesty had not been positive that it would work—but Hardesty had been positive. He was certain that under the circumstances they were creating, the insurance companies would have to pay, and pay promptly. That was Hardesty's best legal advice, and Hardesty had never yet been wrong about a legal matter.

Well—Luther sighed and began to undress—it was done now. He wished that Cosgrove wasn't such a likeable person, but that, unfortunately or otherwise, was necessary. There had to be some reason for getting him out of Sandstone.

He heard Lila's door open, and he paused in the act of removing a shoe. She stopped in the hall, her fur coat over her arm.

"Couldn't sleep, eh?" he said. "Well, I trust you've got something arranged. It's a little late at night for a pick-up."

She smiled weakly, apologetically. "After all, Doc, I *am* human."

"Interesting," he said, letting the shoe drop to the floor. "An interesting if debatable statement."

"You—you don't mind my going out?"

"I don't care what you do."

"I need some money, Doc."

"I'll get it for you in the morning."

"I could take a check . . ."

"You," he said, "can do exactly what you're told. Exactly. Do you understand?"

"I understand," she said, slowly. "Perfectly."

cosgrove 2

It is five o'clock in the morning of my second day here, and I have been lying awake since one.

Excited and happy? I suppose. I suppose that, beneath this bleached mask which does duty as a face, I am still shouting with wonder and delight. But a man can only enjoy so much and then comes sleep.

I wish I had taken nothing to drink on the way here yesterday. I am positive—almost—that I said and did nothing out of the way. And, yet, of course, I cannot be absolutely positive.

I had nodded agreeably when he explained he never drank while driving; and I expressed my gratitude for his understanding of my need to "forget." I drank without urging, and when about a third of the pint was gone, the questions began.

Why had I chosen him to write to? That was simple. The only periodicals we received in the prison were brag-books—"controlled circulation" publications issued for the purpose of squeezing money from individuals and firms who were doing, or hoped to do, business with the politicians in power. I had got his address from a complimentary advertisement in one of these. I had obtained the address of everyone else I appealed to in the same way.

Did I understand why he had put me through that rigamarole with Warden Fish? I was not prepared to question his actions, I said (and quite sincerely), but I believed I understood. He demanded absolute loyalty from his associates. He would have no use for a man who would abandon loyalty for expediency.

Did I have any close relatives or friends? No. I had a married sister who wrote me a brief note each Christmas. At her request, I did not reply. Our only tie was the accident of birth.

What had I read? Everything in the prison library, contributions to which seemed to have stopped about 1920. All of Shakespeare, Dickens, Swift, Twain, Addison and Steele, Rabelais, Schopenhauer, Marx, Scott, Jules Verne, Wilde, Cervantes, Machiavelli, the Rover Boy series, Lewis Carroll, the Bible, the . . .

As I talked, I adjusted the wind-wing on the window next to me until I picked up Dr. Luther's reflection in its nickeled frame. He seemed well pleased with my replies, although, due to three slightly protruding upper teeth, the mere relaxation of his features sometimes gives him the appearance of smiling.

He is about fifty, I should judge, but here, again, it is hard to be certain. His hair is thin and sandy. He is considerably overweight for his height, which is something less than mine. His eyes bulge behind thick-lensed glasses. Add to that a soft voice which switches abruptly from the grammatical and precise to the slangy and vulgar—and you have a man whose age, like himself, is no matter for hasty estimation.

I went on talking and watching him as the miles sped by, knowing that my words were becoming blurred. Knowing, then not knowing . . .

When I awakened hours later, we were only about

ten miles from the city, and the car was turning into a roadhouse near the edge of a large lake.

The establishment had apparently been pretty swank at one time, but that had been a long while ago. It was gone to seed now. We were the only patrons. Looking through the window, I could see why. What I thought was a lake was actually a river—a broad, sluggishly moving expanse of greasy sludge and mud and water; the waste from the city's oil field.

Despite the tightly closed windows and the air-conditioning system, there was a faint and unpleasant smell of sulphur.

"A little present from the oil companies," he said, with a sudden sour laugh. "They've taken a billion dollars out of this field, and they're taking more every day. But they can't afford to dispose of their sludge!"

I didn't say anything, and he laughed again, the same way, staring down at his almost untouched food.

"I should talk," he said, harshly. "Pat, I'm going to lay my cards on the table. Play straight. Tell you something you'd find out in the next twenty-four hours, anyway ..."

"Yes, sir."

"Call me Doc. Everyone does."

"All right, Doc."

"I'm a qualified psychologist, but I haven't practiced in years. I can't give you a job at the clinic because I haven't any. It's just a front for my lobbying. Grafting, in plain English."

I gave him a straight, steady look. "You got me out of Sandstone, Doc," I said. "That's all I need to know about you."

"Well—I'm not apologizing, of course. Hell, they didn't call this state the heart of Balkan America for nothing. When it's a choice of eat or be eaten, what's a sensible man to do?"

"Eat," I said.

He chuckled and made a feinting motion at my chin with his fist. "You'll do, Pat. Now what I had in mind for you was a job with the state—something that won't require any training. How would that suit you?"

"Anything you do will suit me fine," I said. "But—"

"Yes?"

"How can I be of any use to you if I don't work for you?"

"Why should you have to be of any use to me?" His voice was an angry snarl. "Isn't it conceivable that I might want to help you unselfishly? Give you a break when no one else would?"

"I didn't mean to offend you," I said. "I merely hoped to do something in return for what you've done for me."

"Well, skip it," he said. "Maybe we ought to be getting out of here. Later than I thought it was."

He drove slowly, glancing out at the curving river of mud, which, except for its smell, was gradually being lost in the darkness.

3

We passed through the business district, through part of the residential section, and reached the state capital. Its grounds, as you may know, occupy a square mile on the outskirts of the city; the last level land in that neighborhood.

Doc took a street to the south, one leading up a canyon, and, after about a mile, turned in at a house which sat in a cutback against a hillside.

It was a rather old-fashioned, two-story, square-built house, with a long veranda across the front. Except for the ivy-clad trellises, which practically concealed the windows, it seemed out of place in that setting.

Doc drove the car down the driveway and parked it in the one empty stall in the four-stall garage. A couple, a sports roadster, and another sedan—all late models—occupied the others. We walked back down the driveway and around to the front door.

It was standing open, and the lights were on. There was a hall, with rooms on each side, leading straight back to the rear. Glancing up the stairs, I saw that the second floor was arranged the same way.

Doc motioned me to follow him up the stairs.

Upstairs, we stopped in front of the first door on his right. Doc lifted his hand.

Music seeped out to us faintly, and I could hear a man talking in a quiet, hoarse voice and a woman's light laugh.

Doc tapped softly. The talking and the laughter ceased. Then there was a rustling, and the click of a door closing.

"Who's there?"

"Doc."

"Oh." The hoarse voice had an undertone of annoyance.

A key turned in the lock and the door was thrown open.

The man was about fifty, short, rather fat, not dissimilar to Doc in physique. Despite his tousled hair, his drink-flushed face, and the pajamas he was wearing, he looked pompous. He ignored Doc and scowled at me.

"Who the hell are you?" he demanded.

"This is the young man from Sandstone," said Dr. Luther. "Pat, I want you to meet Senator Burkman. The senator was very helpful in getting your release."

Burkman widened his eyes, exaggeratedly, and poked a stubby finger at my chest. "The hell he is," he wheezed. "You can't kid me. He's a fugitive from a country Sunday school, that's what he is."

Doc gave him a very thin smile. Perhaps no smile at all. Those overhung upper teeth were deceptive.

"Well!" said the senator, seizing my hand. "Pat— Pat Cosgrove, isn't it? Glad I could be of service to you. Sorry I couldn't have met you under more auspicious circumstances." He laughed and gave my shoulder a pat.

"I hope I didn't disturb you," said Doc. "I was afraid you might leave before I had a chance to see you. Pat needs a job."

"I thought you were going to give him a job. I've done enough."

"I'm sorry you feel that way," said Doc. "I wonder if there isn't something I could say to change your mind."

He stared at Burkman thoughtfully, the three protruding teeth resting on his lower lip, and Burkman reddened.

"I'd like to, Doc. It's just that I need every job I've got for my own district. I've got a tight race coming up, man! Why not try Flanders, or Dorsey, or Milligan?"

"They have tight races, too."

"Well"—Burkman hesitated, scowling. "Oh, hell. I'll do it. Send him around to the Highway Commission tomorrow."

"Shall I mention your name to Fleming?"

"Yes—no. I'll talk to him myself."

He closed the door quickly, as if he was afraid of being asked for something else. Doc and I went back down the stairs.

He picked up his hat from the bench, inserted a key in the door next to the entrance and waved me inside.

"Dear," he called. "Oh, Lila!" Then, leaving me standing, he strode into the adjoining room, and through the rest of the apartment.

I looked around. To my mind, the room was a little too crowded to be in good taste. There were well-filled bookcases, a piano, and a combination radio-phonograph-television set. There was a long window seat at the front, a longer divan at the opposite side of the room, a chaise longue, and three over-stuffed chairs. In the approximate center of the room was a mirrored coffee table with a built-in flower pot.

Doc returned, slamming the connecting door.

"Mrs. Luther isn't around," he said, harshly. "Not, I suppose, that I really expected her to be. Well—"

A knock on the outer door interrupted him. He flung it open.

"And where," he demanded of the white-jacketed Negro before him, "have you been?"

"With the north suite party, sir." The Negro, a slender, clean-featured youth, smiled placatingly. "One of the gentlemen was a little ill."

"Mrs. Luther leave any message for me?"

"No, sir."

"Huh!" said Doc. "I suppose you have that south rear room ready? Or did you forget about it?"

"I believe it's ready, sir. I mean to say—"

"Come along. You too, Pat."

We went down the hall, Doc striding ahead and the Negro and I following. At the last door to the right, the Negro stepped swiftly to the front, took a brass-tagged key from his pocket and turned the lock. He snapped on the light, and Doc brushed past him.

It was a room such as you might find in any first-class hotel. The few touches of individuality consisted of a small two-bottle bar, with the bottles; a cigarette humidor on a revolving stand, with three kinds of cigarettes; and a magazine rack with a variety of magazines.

Doc switched on the bathroom light and turned on the Negro again.

"Everything all ready, eh?" he said. "What about pajamas, tooth brush, comb, shaving articles? What about socks and underwear and shirts—all that stuff I told you to get?"

"I have them, sir. Everything. I just haven't had time to ..."

"Well, get on it! And get that telephone out of here!

I—" Doc shot me a look of curt apology, "I didn't think you'd want one, Pat."

"Not at all," I said.

He slumped down into a chair and let his head loll back. He removed his glasses, and began wiping them thoughtfully. I felt sorry and embarrassed for him. It is always a little saddening to see a man upset over a woman who, obviously, cares nothing about his feelings.

The Negro unplugged the handset telephone and went out. He returned in a minute or two and began stowing various articles away in the chest of drawers and in the bathroom. Doc had him fix us a drink when he had finished.

"I'm pretty tired tonight, Willie," he said, as he took the glass from the youth's hand. "I'm sorry if I was abrupt."

"That's quite all right, Doctor."

"If Mrs. Luther should return within the next hour, please tell her I'm back here."

"Yes, sir."

The Negro left, closing the door noiselessly. Doc motioned with his glass.

"Well, Pat. Think you can struggle along in here?"

"I don't know about that," I said. "You know how it is at Sandstone. The best of everything and the guest is always right."

He smiled and I told him it wasn't necessary to put himself out so much on my account. I could hole up anywhere, and I'd be just as grateful to him.

"Forget it, Pat," he said. "I haven't anything simplier than this. At any rate, I don't feel inclined to discriminate against my one deserving guest. What did you think of the senator?"

"I'm not forming any opinions," I said. "For the

next two years, at least, I intend to borrow them from you."

"I gather that you mean exactly that."

"I do."

He swished the whiskey around in his glass, staring down into it. "I hope very much, Pat, that everything goes all right. Frankly, you're considerably different from what I'd imagined you'd be. I didn't think that I could develop such a strong personal interest in a—well—"

"Bank robber? I didn't work at the trade long, Doc."

"Of course, I'm glad I have," he went on. "But what I'm trying to say is, I'd take it much harder than I thought I would if anything unpleasant should happen to you."

"Unpleasant?" I said.

"About your parole," he said, with a haste I could not understand. "I suppose you know it wasn't strictly on the level."

I swallowed. Hard. "You mean there's some danger that ...?"

"Now, don't get excited. I just thought I'd warn you that we are in a little hell when we face Myrtle Briscoe tomorrow morning. You know who she is. The State Commissioner of Corrections; also the head of the Parole Board."

"I know," I said. "I hope—"

"Myrtle would let you rot in hell before she'd parole you to me or any of my connections. Willingly. But Myrtle necessarily is sometimes absent from the capital, and, legally, the governor then becomes acting commissioner. He's legally the head of every department during the absence of its nominal head."

"But he's not supposed to use that power?"

"Not except in emergencies which I can't conceive

as arising. It's a serious abridgement of democratic principles. Myrtle's elected—God knows how many times, incidentally—because the people like what she stands for. The governor, who's only in office to get as much as he can, gives them something else."

"What—" I swallowed again, "—what can she do, Doc?"

"I don't want to get you in an uproar, Pat. You seemed like such a cool-headed guy, I thought I could discuss things with you."

"You can," I said. "I'll keep my Sandstone shakes to myself."

"Well, there's nothing she can do. Nothing she will do. Oh, of course, she could go to the newspapers and throw her weight around generally, but the object lesson she'd give us wouldn't be worth the trouble. You're out now. Her tactic will be to take advantage of the fact."

"How can she do that?"

"More ways than I care to think about." He yawned, and eased himself from his chair. "That's my department, though. We'll hear some of them in the morning when we pay our courtesy call."

"Can't we—do we have to see her?" I said.

"Oh, yes. Any kind of delay would be very dangerous. Moreover, I imagine you'll have to see her every month during the term of your parole. I don't think she'd trust a case like you to a run-of-the-mill probation officer."

"Well," I said. "Forewarned, forearmed."

He chuckled and moved toward the door. "That's better. I'm glad to see I was right about you. A worrier could be very annoying."

"I understand," I said. "I'll try not to bother you."

"Well, don't get corked up. You'll need a lot of help

in getting squared away and I'm glad to give it. I just don't want you upsetting yourself and me with senseless fretting."

We said goodnight.

I began to undress, wondering what made him tick, and why the ticks were as they were. It settled down to who he really was—the threatening, cold-eyed man who had bullied Burkman, or the man who had been angry over the pollution of a river and ashamed of being part of the general pattern of pollution.

Whichever was the case, one thing was certain: he was a considerable improvement over Warden Fish. Whatever happened to me, nothing could be worse than being back in Sandstone. I would be better off dead than there.

I went to sleep on that thought.

4

The little alarm clock at my bedside went off at seven, and after I had showered and was shaving, another white-jacketed Negro wheeled in a breakfast cart.

He introduced himself as Henry, and made a polite but reserved mention of the fact that he was Willie's brother. He was in and out of the room in five minutes, including the time it took to remove the silver covers from the dishes, fill my cup with coffee, and prop a morning paper against the pot.

I slipped into my clothes and sat down at the table.

Doc's cook, apparently, was as topnotch as his other servants. There were tiny hot biscuits; sectioned grapefruit packed in shaved ice; oatmeal cooked so that each flake was separate from the others; and a golden and puffy bacon omelet that was almost light enough to float.

Doc had me drive his sedan into town. I was a little reluctant to try it but he insisted, and it was easy enough after I got used to the steering-wheel gear shift.

I hadn't been in Capital City since my senior year in high school. At that time it had been a big sprawling town with a great many parks, clean wide streets, and modest, comfortable appearing homes. Now the streets were jammed and dirty; two and sometimes three shacks stood on a lot once occupied by a single neat cottage; and the parks were islands of oil well derricks, surrounded by barbed-wire fences. There were fine homes, certainly; some of them occupying an entire block with their wide, well-kept lawns. But they pointed up, rather than detracted from, the general picture of decay and squalor.

I put the car on a parking lot Doc directed me to, and we sat there several minutes while he turned through the paper. At last he folded it carelessly, tossed it into the back seat and took out his wallet.

"Here's forty dollars, Pat. It'll give you something to rattle until payday."

"I—"

"I know. You're grateful. And you hope to show your appreciation. And if I see an opportunity for you to do so, for this or any other favor, past or impending, I'll let you know. Anything else?"

"I was going to thank you," I said, "but I guess I'd better not."

"You just have. Now let's see about some clothes."

We crossed the street and walked up to the corner where he led me to the entrance of a store.

A tall gray-haired man in a black coat and striped pants strolled out to us.

"Ah, Doctor," he said. "I hope we're to be allowed to serve you in some way?"

Doc shook hands with him indifferently. "I think I'll let you take care of my friend," he said. "This is Mr. Cosgrove, Williams."

"It will be a pleasure," Williams beamed, giving my hand a tender shake. He didn't seem to notice my clothes.

"Mr. Cosgrove has been ill for a long time," Doc

went on. "He'll need a complete outfitting, but we have an appointment within the hour. Can you fix him up in something casual immediately, and get his measurements for a couple of suits and whatever he needs in the way of accessories? Send it out to the house later."

"Certainly," said Williams. "We'll be very prompt with Mr. Cosgrove. Now, if I may show you inside . . ."

Doc hesitated a moment, studying a tweed sports coat. He half turned and started to enter the store, then he glanced across the street. He stiffened.

"I won't be able to go in," he said quickly. "Meet me at the car when you're through, Pat. Williams, I'm putting Mr. Cosgrove in your hands."

"Thank you, Doctor."

"He'll use my account."

"Of course, Doctor. If you please, Mr. Cosgrove."

Doc swung off across the street, moving in quick angry strides. I let Williams lead me into the store.

The next thirty minutes were like a comedy. Shoes were being slid on and off my feet while my shoulders were draped and undraped with coats. I tried on trousers while hats were being placed on my head. A swarm of frock-coated salesmen moved around me with coats, pants, ties and shirts, hats and shoes. And Williams said "Quite," and "Exactly," and "I'm afraid not."

Then they were all gone except Williams and a clerk, who was fitting a linen handkerchief into my breast pocket while Williams turned me toward a three-view mirror.

"I don't see how you did it," I said, at last. And it is hard to say who felt the better about it, they or I.

Williams escorted me to the entrance and we shook hands again. I crossed the street to the parking lot.

It had filled up considerably by this time, and there were cars on both sides of Doc's. I didn't know there was anyone with him until I was almost behind the sedan. Then, the door slammed and I heard the other man curse.

"You're being a fool!" he said. "You'll spoil everything with your damned jealousy!"

"Don't give me cause to be jealous, then," Doc snarled. "She's my wife. You'd better remember that."

"I've told you it was simply business!"

"Business or not—"

"To hell with you! Try pulling something and see how far you get!"

The man came bounding out of the lane between the two cars, head down, blind with rage. I bumped into him, bringing my heel down on his instep. When he doubled, I let him have a touch of elbow across the windpipe.

I had to grab him then to keep him from keeling over.

5

He was a handsome, forty-ish sort; dark, keen-eyed, bold looking. I could see why Mrs. Luther might like him. I felt an instinctive, almost unwilling liking for him myself. I'd given him a jolt, but after one murderous glance he was trying to grin.

Doc got out and helped hold him up, and he looked at me as though he wasn't too well-pleased.

"Are you all right, Bill?" he said. "Can I do something?"

The man shook his head. "Just—just give me a second. I'll come out of it."

"You shouldn't have done that, Pat," said Doc. "It was entirely unnecessary."

"I'm sorry," I said. "It was an accident."

"Well, it might have been very serious. From what I saw—"

"Oh, stop bawling him out!" The man straightened up, and spoke in a normal tone. "Pat thought you were in trouble and tried to help you. Now cut out the scolding and introduce me."

"Of course," said Doc. "Mr. Hardesty, Pat Cosgrove. Mr. Hardesty is an attorney, Pat. He was instrumental in obtaining your release from Sandstone."

Another one, I thought. How many, how much, why . . . ?

"And I was glad to have the chance!" Hardesty wrung my hand. "They gave you a mighty raw deal, son. I'm glad to see you came through it so well."

"Thank you very much," I said.

"My pleasure entirely. I like the cut of your jib, Pat. I like to see a man who sticks up for his friends." His warm dark eyes traveled over me admiringly. "He looks like a million dollars, doesn't he, Doc?"

"Pat and I have got to be going," said Doc. "We've got to see the Commissioner of Corrections about Pat's parole."

"Mad Myrtle, huh?" Hardesty chuckled. "Can't say that I envy you. If she gives you too much trouble—"

"I think I can handle her," said Doc.

"If you can't, she can't be handled," Hardesty agreed. He grinned, nodded to me and strolled away whistling. I crawled in at Doc's side and headed the car toward the capitol.

He was silent for several blocks, seemingly absorbed in his newspaper. Finally, he repeated an action that was to become familiar to me—folded and tossed the newspaper over his shoulder—and spoke:

"What did you hear of my conversation with Hardesty?"

"Not very much," I said.

"I asked you what you heard."

"Well, I heard you tell him to keep away from Mrs. Luther, and he swore and said you were just jealous."

Doc turned in the seat and I felt the full power of the gaze that raged out through the thick-lensed glasses. Yet something—something I implausibly sensed as fear—held back the explosion.

"Perhaps I didn't make myself clear, Pat," he said softly. "You've got an excellent memory; I've tested it on several occasions. Now! Give me a word for word account of what you heard."

I did it. I repeated it word for word.

"And what do you make of that, Pat? Any questions you'd like to ask?"

"I don't make anything of it," I said. "I haven't any questions."

Doc settled back in the seat. He laughed quietly.

"Hardesty's a nice fellow," he said, "but he's a little too quick to fly off the handle. You rather cooled him off."

"I'm sorry about that," I said. "I thought you might want him so I tried to stop him for you."

"And I appreciated it." He put his hand on my knee for a moment. "However, it wasn't necessary, as you know now. Hardesty and I are actually pretty good friends," he went on. "Mrs. Luther fell heir to a small estate some time ago and he's been handling it for her. He's the kind of man that can't talk to anyone, male or female, without getting personal; and I should have known he didn't mean anything by his attitude toward Mrs. Luther. But I'm afraid I'm not very reasonable where she's concerned."

"I understand."

"Well, let's forget it," he said. "You did an excellent job on your clothing, Pat. I had to look twice to recognize you."

"Williams should get the credit for that," I said.

"I'll give it to him." He smiled at me in the mirror. "I'll also give him credit for the bill—just in case you were worrying about it."

"It's nice to hear you say so," I said.

"Don't give it another thought," he said. "Well, here we are."

I parked in one of the drives on the capitol grounds proper, and we walked across a stretch of lawn, and started up the marble steps of the main entrance.

We pushed our way through the crowded corridors, Doc speaking and being spoken to occasionally, and took a jerkily-moving elevator to the fourth and top floor—"Renegades' Roost," Doc whispered, as we stepped off the car.

We turned off the central corridor, and wound through a series of narrow hallways. Just when I was beginning to believe Doc was lost, we came to a door marked:

DEPARTMENT OF CORRECTIONS
Myrtle Briscoe
Commissioner

Doc threw away his cigarette and removed his hat. Mine was already in my hand. He gave his tie a final pat, straightened his shoulders and opened the door.

6

A hatchet-faced girl with greasy hair and horn-rimmed glasses was pecking away at a typewriter.

She looked up when we came in, started to smile—and made a point of changing her mind. The nostrils of her oily nose quivered.

"Well!" she said.

"How do you do?" said Doc. "Will you please tell Miss Briscoe that Dr. Luther and Mr. Cosgrove are here."

"I certainly will!" snapped the girl. "And how!"

She got up, walked over to a door marked "Private" and knocked. She opened it and stuck her head inside.

"Miss Briscoe, *Doctor* Luther and *Mister* Cosgrove are here to—"

A roar cut her off. "So he showed up, did he? Well, lock the vault and send him in! Send 'em both in!"

The girl turned, flushed, smiling meanly.

"Come right in—*gentlemen.*"

We went in, and the girl closed the door behind us.

I imagine every convict and ex-convict in the country has heard of Myrtle Briscoe. She'd held an elective office in a politicians' graveyard for thirty years, and remained honest.

She was about five feet tall, including the red

discolored topknot of her hair. She wore a white shirtwaist with a high collar, high-topped button shoes, and a skirt that resembled a horse blanket.

She stood up, as we entered, but she didn't offer to shake hands. "Sit down there," she snapped. "No, no! Keep your chairs together. I want you birds where I can watch you!"

Doc said, "Really, Miss Briscoe. Is that—"

"Shut up!" she bellowed. "Shut your big bazoo and keep it shut until I tell you to open it! Cosgrove, where did you get those clothes? You look like a pawnshop salesman."

"Miss Briscoe," said Doc. "I will not tolerate—"

"Will you shut up! Cosgrove?"

"Doctor Luther bought them for me."

"Why?"

"It's too cold to go without any," I said. "And the state fund for buying them seems to be exhausted."

"So?" She leaned back in her chair, eyes glinting. "Any idea why it is exhausted?"

"No, ma'am," I said. "But *I've* been in prison for fifteen years."

She chuckled sourly. "All right, young Cosgrove; I stepped into that one. Now, I'm going to tell you the secret behind that non-existent state fund. I'm going to tell you why you don't have any money to buy books at Sandstone; why the food is slop. Why this, one of the richest states in the union, has become a begger among the other commonwealths ..."

"I'm sorry, Miss Briscoe," I said. "I didn't mean—"

"It's because we're eaten up by rats. Rats, do you understand? That's the only name for them. And I don't give a damn how nicely they dress and talk or how generous—generous, hell!—they are to people who play along with 'em.

"Who else but rats would foist inferior textbooks upon children; force an entire generation to grow up in ignorance? Who else would take money at the cost of leaving dangerous highways unrepaired? Who else would build firetraps for helpless old men and women? Who else would place two thousand men in the care of a maniac to be starved and tortured, yes, and killed? Well? What do you say, Cosgrove? You, of all people, ought to agree with me."

"I read the Brookings Institution report," I said.

"Oh, you did? Well, well! But what did you do when my investigators were there at Sandstone? Did you talk to them, tell them exactly what you were up against?"

"No, ma'am," I said.

"No. You're damned right you didn't! You expect one woman with the lowest budget of—"

"But I know some that did talk," I said.

"Oh," she said flatly; and for a full minute she was silent. Then she sighed, scowled, and looked at Doc. "Doctor, why wasn't the application for Cosgrove's parole made in the usual way?"

"I, uh—" Doc hesitated, drawing his lip down over the protruding teeth. "Senator Burkman thought that—"

"Senator Burkman never had a thought in his life, and you can tell him I said so! You were confident I wouldn't parole anyone to you, weren't you? Oh, don't bother to answer. Where will Cosgrove be employed? In that brothel of yours?"

"Miss Briscoe," said Doc, dangerously. "I don't care for your language."

"Woof, woof," Myrtle Briscoe grinned. "Well?"

"I plan on getting him a job with the state. Of course, he's technically in my employ until—"

"I know. I know the routine. And you, Cosgrove, you're willing to be another hog at the public trough?"

I smiled at her, and she grimaced wryly.

"Foolish question, huh? Doc give you any reason for all this dough he's blowing on you?"

"Whatever is spent on me," I said, "I intend to pay back."

"How?" She spoke as though Doc were not in the room. "Any idea what a caper of this kind costs, Red? Hardesty was in on it. So was Burkman. So were the several legislators he horsetraded into bringing pressure on the governor."

"Miss Briscoe—"

"Doc, if you don't shut up I'll put you out of the office. . . . So that's your picture, Red, or most of it. I don't mean that Doc spent much actual cash in getting you out. What he and his crowd spent were pledges. They tacitly cancelled certain favors owing them and obligated themselves for others. They used up a lot of their steam—steam they could use right now. Now, why do you think they did that, Red?"

"I know why," I said. "But I'd prefer that Doc explained it to you."

"Smart," she said, eyes narrowed. "Can you cook, too?"

"Miss Briscoe," said Doc. "I want you to believe I helped Pat for just one reason: because he needed help and deserved it, and I was in a position to give it."

"I know you want me to believe that."

"Pat served fifteen years for a robbery in which nothing was lost and no one was hurt. He served it not because he was a criminal, but because he wasn't. He should never have been sent to anything but a juvenile correctional institution."

"You're right there," said Miss Briscoe, grudgingly.

"Pat stayed on in Sandstone five years after he was eligible for parole. Ten years would have been a terrible punishment, but he stayed five years more. He could have spent his whole life there, solely because he had no friends or money."

"And you got him out, solely out of the goodness of your heart."

"Put it this way," said Doc, slowly. "I've—I've made a lot of mistakes. Maybe this will help wipe some of them out."

Myrtle Briscoe stared at him, elbows on her desk, hands under her chin.

"Dammit, Doc, I'd like to believe that!"

"It's the truth."

"Maybe. Maybe not. I've lived so much of my life surrounded by crooks that—" She broke off. "Pat—Red, Sandstone isn't a very nice place, is it?"

"Suppose I said yes," I said. "Or no?"

"Never mind. But there's more than one kind of prison, Red. They don't all have walls around them."

"I know," I said. "I worked in the library, Miss Briscoe."

"Well, I hope you learned something. You've had a bad time. I hope you're not in for something worse. Not that it makes much difference. I'm like everyone else; I have to play ball. Doc knew I would, didn't you, Doc?"

"I hoped for your cooperation, certainly, Miss Briscoe."

"I'll play—this time. But don't get in a rut, Doc. There's an election coming up, and I'm pretty sick of trying to clean house with a whiskbroom."

Myrtle Briscoe came around the desk and gripped me by both arms and looked up into my face.

"I was kidding about the clothes," she said. "You

look good—and you're going to have to be good. Hard as it may be, and even if we both think it's nonsense. You know what I mean. No drunks, no wild women, no rough stuff. That's what the books say. That's what I say as long as they say it."

"Yes, ma'am," I said.

"Maybe," she said. "Maybe—oh, get the hell out of here!"

7

There was a restaurant in the basement of the capitol, and Doc and I ate lunch there. Neither of us was very hungry, and we had only a salad, rolls and a bottle of ale each.

Several people stopped by our table. There was a Senator Flanders with a man who, as nearly as I could make out, was a textbook salesman. There was a commissioner of something-or-other whose name I didn't catch. Another senator named Kronup. Several people; I saw them all later, from time to time, around Doc's house.

Burkman came in, just as we were finishing the ale, and took a chair at our table. There were pouches under his eyes, and his voice was even more hoarse than it had been the night before.

Doc told him about Myrtle Briscoe.

"Myrtle dropped a hint about not running next time. A threat, rather."

"Nonsense! I happen to know she's already lining up her campaign material. Anyway, she doesn't need to run. She'd get a big enough write-in vote to be elected."

Burkman cursed. "It'd be about like the old bitch to pull something like that! We're going to have to baby her along a little bit, Doc. Get her some better offices. Let her have another investigator."

"It might not be a bad idea."

"You'd better tour around with me this afternoon, Doc. I want you to tell the governor—" Burkman paused, looking from me to Doc. "I meant to tell you, Pat; I got that job for you. Drop around to the Highway Commission tomorrow morning and ask for Mr. Fleming."

"Thank you, very much," I said. "About what time, Senator?"

"Oh, suit yourself. Some time in the forenoon."

"What does it pay?" Doc asked.

"Two and a half. Best I could do right now."

Doc shrugged. "It could be worse. What about it, Pat? Do you think you can accept a job at two hundred and fifty a month?"

"I'm very grateful," I said. "I only hope I'll be able to do the work."

Burkman's eyes widened. Then, he leaned back and roared with laughter. Doc chuckled. "The job won't be too difficult," he said pointedly, reaching for our check. "I'm going to be tied up for the next couple of hours. Is there anything you'd like to do?"

"Why, nothing in particular," I said. "I wouldn't mind strolling around the building."

"That's a good idea; give the people a chance to see what the well-dressed man is wearing. Come back here and have something more to eat or drink if you like."

"I think I'll just walk around," I said. "Where shall I meet you?"

"Oh," he glanced at his watch, "make it the front entrance."

I said I'd be there, shook hands with the senator, and left.

It took me almost an hour to find the state historical museum. Most of the cases and cabinets were empty. Tacked on the front of them were small, age-yellowed signs:

EXHIBIT ON TEMPORARY LOAN

I went from the museum to the state library— "Closed For Repairs." Then, since my time was running short, I located the highway commission offices and went out to the entrance to wait for Doc.

I was leaning against the stone balustrade and starting to light a cigarette when she came out.

I dislike trying to describe her, because the physical facts of a person so seldom add up to what that person really is.

She was no youngster—every line of her full but compact body spoke the mature woman—and she made no attempt to appear one, superficial facts to the contrary. She was just herself, a forever young and gay self, and I could not picture her as acting or dressing in any other way than she did.

She wore a plain blue dress with a white collar and a little white belt, tied in the back. She wore low-heeled shoes, and I think her firm round legs were bare. She had a black straw hat with a saucer-like brim which was slung over her arm by its elastic band. Her crisp brown hair was pulled back in a single thick curl, barely reaching to her shoulders and tied with a tiny white ribbon.

She stood at the top of the steps for a minute, breathing deeply, happily; her brown eyes and her small straight nose, her entire face crinkling with good humor. She smiled at me, without actually seeing me, of course: impersonally, simply because it was a nice day and she was alive and that was good.

Then, she went jauntily down the steps, the hat swinging over her arm, the little belt spanking her gently on her bottom.

I wanted to run after her, ask her name, hold her somehow; never let her go away. And I remembered who I was—Doc—Myrtle Briscoe—Sandstone—and I could only stand and watch. Feeling sick and empty. Lost.

Near the end of the walk she stepped over into the driveway, and started down the row of parked cars.

She stopped at Doc's big black sedan, glanced casually over her shoulder and opened the door.

I stood where I was for a moment, unable or unwilling to believe what I had seen. Then, I went down the steps, three at a time. I cut across the driveway and ran, stooping, along the far row of cars. I came parallel with Doc's sedan, vaulted silently over a bumper and dropped down behind her.

She was kneeling on the seat of the car, her back— well, not her *back,* exactly—to me. She pulled a zipper on the seat cover, reached in between the cover and the seat, and fumbled for a moment. She brought out a long, thick brown envelope.

She put a foot down on the running board, and started to back out. I was in the way. She wiggled a little, not realizing that someone was behind her. She pushed, and I pushed back.

She looked around, then.

"Oh," she gasped, and her mouth dropped open. Then, the crinkled smile returned and she cocked her head on one side. "Now, really," she said, in a teasing-scolding tone. "Don't you think you should ask a girl, first?"

I backed off a step, feeling my face go red. "I'm with

Dr. Luther," I said, nodding at the car. "I saw you take something . . . that envelope."

"Nooo!" Her mouth formed an *o* of exaggerated awe. "What do people call you, you pretty red-haired man?"

"My name is Cosgrove," I said. "Patrick Cosgrove. And I'll take that envelope."

"Bet you won't," she said, instantly, her eyes dancing.

"Now, look, Miss—"

"Flournoy. Madeline Flournoy."

"You say that like it should mean something to me," I said. "But it doesn't. I'm afraid—"

"I work for Doc. He sent me after these contracts. Now is that good enough for you, or do you want to wrestle?"

"If you work for Doc," I said, "you won't mind my walking back with you to where he is."

"I don't mind at all, Patsy," she said promptly. "But I've made it a lifelong principle never to give in to a redhead."

"I'm sorry," I said. "I'll either have to go with you or have you wait here until Doc comes."

She put the papers and her hat behind her, lowered her head and walked right into me. She pushed against me and I could hear her teeth gritting.

I tried to reach around her and grab the papers. Instead, I caught hold of her hat, breaking the band that held it to her arm. It struck the running board and rolled between us.

"Now see what you did," she said, reproachfully.

"I'm sorry," I said.

We both reached for it at the same time. Our heads bumped painfully. It gave me a bad jolt, and I know it must have hurt her worse. Her face went momentarily white.

I said I was sorry again, and started to pick up the hat.

She brought her knee against my chin with a force that almost knocked me out.

It was instinctive, a natural animal reaction to pain. What I did was also instinctive.

I grabbed her by the ankles and jerked upward.

She sailed through the door of the car, open fortunately, and landed bouncing on the seat. Her feet went up in the air and her dress flew over her head.

"Just what the hell," said Dr. Luther, "is going on here?"

8

His hat was jammed low on his sandy hair, and there was a fleck of spittle beneath the overhung teeth. He pushed me to one side and almost jerked her off the seat.

"What in the name of God is the matter with you, Madeline?" he said harshly. "I sent you after those contracts thirty minutes ago, and I waited and waited until my parties gave up and left. And then I come out here and find you showing your backside to—to—"

"Was not backside," she pouted. "Was underneath side."

"To hell with that stuff! You're not a kid; you're not being paid kid's wages! If you can't snap out of it and do your work like you're supposed to, I'll get someone who will."

"Bet you couldn't!" she said. "Bet you couldn't get any one that knows," she stressed the word ever so lightly, "half as much as I do."

"But, dammit!" He stared at her helplessly, swallowing whatever else he had been about to say.

"It's my fault, Doc," I said. "I saw her get those papers out of the car, and I jumped to the wrong conclusion."

"And I was nasty to him," said Madeline, "in my own peculiar way."

"I can imagine," Doc said. "Well, I guess I'm as much at fault as anyone. I'd forgotten about Pat waiting there at the entrance. By the way, you two had better meet each other."

He introduced us, casually, and opened the door of the car. "Make another copy of those contracts tonight, Madeline," he said. "And bring them out here in the afternoon. Same place. Same time. *On* time!"

"I was going to a show tonight."

"Go ahead. Get up early in the morning and work. I don't care when you do them."

"Well—" she stood near the door, pouting. And with her left hand she scrawled an address in the dust on the car's side and wrote "4-noon" beneath it. "Well, you and Mr. Cosgrove can drive me home, then."

"We've something important to do," said Doc, coolly. "Come along, Pat."

I rubbed out the writing, nodded to her, and walked on around the car. As I drove away, she put her hands behind her and stuck her tongue out at Doc.

"That woman," he muttered. "If she wasn't so valuable to me . . ."

"She's your secretary?"

"Call her that. She's actually a great deal more; does things that aren't ordinarily included in secretarial work. She knows—well, you heard her. She knows."

"I see," I said.

"There's a perfect example of what being sorry for a person can get you into," he went on, wearily. "When I first ran into her I thought she was one of the most pitiable, helpless little tykes that ever came out of business college. Raised by an aunt who kicked her out when she was sixteen— I can understand why, now! Worked her way through school as a waitress with all the big bad men insulting her. Just wanted to work real hard for a nice fatherly man like me who would give her good advice. Well . . ."

I laughed appreciatively. "Isn't she a pretty disrupting influence to have around?"

"She gets on my nerves plenty, yes. But she's smart and fast, and people like her in spite of themselves. They let their guards down around her before they realize she's not half as giddy as she appears to be. She—"

"Excuse me, Doc," I said. "Where did you want to drive to?"

"Why, home, I suppose. Unless you've got some place you'd like to go."

"Not at all," I said. "I just thought I understood you to say that—"

"That was a brush-off. I have to use her in my business. I don't have to cart her around—give her any kind of a personal hold on me. Incidentally, Pat . . ."

"Yes," I said, knowing what was coming.

"I want you to keep away from her, too. I know you're loyal and grateful to me, that you wouldn't deliberately do anything that might injure me. But it's simply a bad idea for two people so close to my affairs to get on an intimate basis. You understand, Pat? I won't tolerate it."

He turned to look at me. I nodded emphatically, not trusting my voice.

He said, "I'm counting on you."

I let him out at the front of the house, and drove the car on back to the garage.

Then another car—the sports roadster I'd seen the night before—swept down the driveway. It shot into the stall next to the sedan, tires sliding, and banged noisily, but apparently harmlessly, against the rear of the garage.

A woman got out and came swiftly toward me, smiling, hand extended.

She was above average height, and slender, yet there was a soft billowy look about her. Her hair was ash blonde, and she had the smooth flawless complexion which should, but so seldom does, accompany it. She wore a tailored, fawn-colored suit with a fox fur scarf around the shoulders.

Briefly, she was a very beautiful woman of thirty or thereabouts. A little theatrical in her actions, but beautiful. And absolutely nothing else.

"You're Pat Cosgrove," she announced, dipping her hand a little to take hold of mine. "Doctor's told me so much about you. I'm Lila Luther."

"How do you do, Mrs. Luther," I said.

"I was going to drop in last night and say hello, but Doctor said you were tired And, of course, he snatched you away this morning before I got my eyes open."

"Well ..." I said.

"Do come along." She linked her wrist over my arm. "I want you to show me your room. Doctor assured me you were made utterly comfortable, but naturally he wouldn't know if you weren't. Isn't he a weird man? But sweet. Very sweet."

"I like him," I said, trying not to make it sound like a reproof. "And the room is fine. I—"

"Oh, well," she shrugged. "Of course, you *would* like him. Not that you're not sincere. I could see instantly that you were. Do you know Mr. Hardesty? I like him very much, don't you? He's such a smooth, earnest man. So, uh, so unweird."

She chattered incessantly as we went up the

driveway and around the walk to the house, apparently so intrigued with the sound of her own voice that my tense silence went unnoticed.

At the door of her apartment, hers and Doc's, she rapped briskly and called:

"Doctor! I'll be with Mr. Cosgrove for a few minutes!"

Then, without waiting for a reply, she urged me down the hall, her long, soft thigh brushing against mine.

I unlocked the door of my room, and pushed it open for her. She took my arm and we went in together.

"Well," she said, glancing around critically. "They haven't done *too* badly by you."

"It's far better than anything I've had," I said. "There's really nothing I need, Mrs. Luther."

"Nothing at all?" She gave my arm a sly squeeze. "Well I do. I need a drink."

"Mrs. Luther," I said. "Do—do you—"

"What?" She raised one delicate, glossy eyebrow. "Oh some of that bourbon will be all right. With just a little water, please."

I nodded and went over to the bar—hearing the door ease shut almost the moment my back was turned.

Doc would resent my ordering her out. No matter what he might think about her himself, he would resent anyone else's implication that she was less than she could be. I could only hope he would not let jealousy get the better of his common sense. Surely, he must realize that I would not play loose with his wife.

I mixed the drink and brought it over to her. I lighted her cigarette. I tried not to notice as she toed off her highheeled suede slippers.

"Do sit down, Pat," she said. Then, "Oh, where's your drink?"

"I don't drink very much, Mrs. Luther," I said. "I don't think I want one just now."

"But I never drink alone! I mean, I'm very serious about it!"

"Mrs. Luther ..."

"Lila. Or don't you like the name?"

"I like it very much, but—"

"Say it, then."

"Lila," I said flatly.

What happened then was so completely insane that I am almost doubtful it did happen.

She set her glass on the floor and arose, letting the fox scarf slide from her shoulders. She put her arms around me and turned, turning me, and slumped backwards. She went down on the bed, drawing me down with her.

Her eyes were closed and she was breathing deeply, and her head rocked a little from side to side on its thick pallet of ash blonde hair ... Her lips parted and she raised them up toward mine. And, almost, I bent down to them. I wanted to. I wanted her.

I believe it must have been the red of her mouth which brought me to my senses. Lipstick: evidence: penalty. Or perhaps I heard the soft footsteps in the thickly carpeted hallway ... although that does not seem possible.

Whatever the case was, I did not bend down.

I reversed the trick she had pulled on me.

I moved up and backwards, swiftly, jerking her upright before she could release her hold. I caught her by the elbows, literally swung her in an arc, and dropped her into the chair. I swept the hair back from her face. I dropped the scarf around her shoulders. I slipped the shoes on her feet and thrust the glass into her hand.

I made a leap for the door.

It was locked. She had turned the latch.

I turned it again, turning the knob noisily at the same time.

As I did so, I felt it turn from the other side; and Dr. Luther walked in.

9

"Oh," I said. "I was going to call you, Doc. Mrs. Luther thought you might have time for a drink with us."

He shook his head curtly, and looked at her. He looked her over very carefully. "Are you through with that drink yet?"

"It doesn't look like it, does it?"

"Drink it up, then. Or take it with you."

She stared at him, smiling in a funny way, swinging one long perfect leg.

"Lila," he said, a note of apology in his voice. "Don't you think ... ?"

"I'll tell you what I think," she said, arising. "I think you'd better take it." And she hurled the contents of the glass squarely into his face.

I wanted to slap her. I hoped, no matter what happened to me, that Doc would. Instead, he merely stood there helplessly, the whiskey dripping down from his glasses, running in little rivulets toward his mouth and chin.

Mrs. Luther laughed shortly. She turned and gave me a bright, vacant smile.

"Sorry about the carpet, Pat," she said; and she strolled out of the room, closing the door behind her.

"Doc," I said. "Doc ..."

He turned and looked at me, slowly, his glasses misted over by the whiskey. He made a pawing motion at them with one hand.

"Doc," I said again, helplessly, and he took a hesitating step toward me.

He took another step and I moved out of the way. He went past me and into the bathroom, and I heard water being turned on. I went over to the bar and poured myself a stiff drink, straight. I was tilting the bottle for the second time when the bathroom door opened.

"Make that two, will you, Pat?" said Doc, casually.

"Certainly," I said, and I poured another one, trying to keep the bottle from rattling against the glass.

He'd washed and tidied himself up, and he looked pretty much the same as he always had. The terrific inner strain was apparent only in the tight line of his mouth, the unconsciously self-conscious way in which he kept his lips drawn over the protruding teeth.

He sat down in one of the upholstered chairs. I handed him a glass and sat down across from him.

"Well," he smiled at me almost timidly, "here's how, Pat."

"How," I said. And then I banged the glass down, slopping whiskey onto the coffee table.

"Dammit to hell, Doc," I said, "I'm going to tell you a few things. You may not like—"

"Don't bother, Pat. I don't think you can tell me anything I don't already know."

"You can't know, or—"

"Yes. Yes, I can know, all right, and still not accept. Fight against accepting. I think it might be better if I told you a few things about myself. When you know them you can understand about Lila."

"You don't need to explain anything to me, Doc," I said. "I—"

"I should have done it before. You'll be hearing things from other people, and you may as well get the straight story from me ... Do you recall one of Myrtle Briscoe's opening remarks this morning—the one about locking the vault?"

"Why," I nodded, "yes."

"That little barb was intended for me, Pat. You and I have at least one thing in common."

"You mean that—that you robbed a bank, too?"

"Just a safe, a vault in the college where I was an instructor." He smiled wryly and shook his head. "I made about as big a botch of it as you did, even though I didn't go to prison. I sometimes wonder whether that was a break, whether I wouldn't have been better off if ..."

"No," I said. "No one's better off for that."

"It's something I'll never know, I guess. How about another drink?"

I got the bottle and brought it over to the table. He added a little to the drink I poured for him, and took most of it at a swallow. He shuddered and smacked his lips.

"It happened about ten years ago, Pat," he said, abruptly breaking into speech. "I was about your age, a few years older, perhaps, and my prospects didn't look half as good. I'd scraped and starved and slaved through the best years of my life to get an education—and all I'd got out of it was an assistant professorship in a jerkwater college. It would be years, I knew, before I got any more than that; before I became a full professor and finally, if I was lucky, a department head. The last thing I should have done, from a practical standpoint, was to get married. I got married, anyway."

He took another drink, glancing at me over the rim

of his glass. "I see the full significance of that escapes you, Pat. You can't understand what it means to have income staked at a definite and unchangeable level, and to take on an obligation which far exceeds it. We didn't plan it that way, of course. Lila was a student of mine, working her way through as I had. We were going to keep the thing secret until she finished school and I—or the two of us together—was making enough to establish a home. That's the way we planned it.

"What happened was, she became pregnant. She had to quit school and her part-time job. She had to have money and she was going to have to have more when the baby came and afterward. I got it for her one day . . . when the registrar was out of his office and the safe was standing open."

"Doc," I said, when he had been silent for several seconds. "Are you sure you want to tell me all this?"

"I—I think so." He rubbed his eyes. "About the money. It didn't take them long to discover it was missing nor to prove that I'd taken it. I admitted it—said I'd lost it gambling. They let me resign and the police gave me twenty-four hours to get out of town.

"I didn't dare go near Lila; I was afraid even to send her a message. She had to have that money, you see. *Had* to have it.

"I came here, about as far away from the other place as I could get. I rented an office on credit and slept on the floor at night, and fixed my own meals whenever I had the money to buy food. Inside of a year I'd built up a pretty fair practice as a consulting psychologist, so I sent for her. I'd only written her one other letter before that. I hadn't signed it or given any address, and I was afraid to say much except that I was well and she wasn't to worry.

"Well, she came here, Pat. Alone. I'll never forget the look on her face when I asked her where the baby was. I—you see—she thought I'd abandoned her. All those months she'd thought that. The baby had been born dead."

"I'm sorry, Doc," I said. "After all, though, it wasn't your fault."

"I'm afraid you and I aren't the best judges of that, Pat," he said, slowly. "We're not equipped to judge . . . anything about her. Well. Want to hear the rest of the story?"

"If you don't mind telling it."

"There's not much more. I'd had to use my own name to establish my right to practice, so it didn't take long for my past to catch up with me. People found out who I was.

"They found out—but just a little late. A psychologist learns things that could be embarrassing, and there's an unusual number of such things to be learned around a state capitol. When the professional groups began cracking down on me, I was already in. I had to agree to stop practicing, but I was in. I've stayed in."

"And you wish you were out?" I said.

"Naturally." He shrugged. "I've never belonged in this game any more than you belonged in Sandstone. Aside from the fact that I'm constantly forced to go against all my instincts and training, I just don't fit. I don't know my way around. I had the few original contacts, and I've used this place to get more. But I've had to depend on people like, well, our friend Hardesty to steer me. Being dependent upon anyone in a game of this kind has serious disadvantages."

"Yes," I said. "I can see that it would."

He stretched lazily and stood up, frowning absently at the small clock on the writing table. "Well, I'll run along now. I didn't mean to stay so long, but I thought I'd put your mind at rest about a few things."

And on that seemingly commonplace remark, Dr. Ronald Luther, ex-professor of psychology turned lobbyist, left the room.

Henry brought in my dinner and cleaned up the mess on the carpet. I ate, unpacked the clothes that had come from the store, and tried to read a while. I couldn't. I went to bed; sleep wouldn't come.

Doc came in the next morning while I was finishing my coffee, and sat down on the bed. He asked me if I'd slept well, and said the new suit looked nice on me. I made the proper replies. Not much was said after that until we reached the capitol.

We were starting up the long steps of the main entrance when he cleared his throat, with a trace of embarrassment, and spoke.

"I know you're as anxious to avoid unfavorable impressions as I am. If Mrs. Luther should visit your room again, it might be best to leave the door open."

"What?" I said, and turned in my tracks and looked at him. "But, Doc—"

I didn't finish the sentence, although it was an effort to choke it off. The look of stubborn embarrassment on his face stopped me. He'd convinced himself all over again that Lila couldn't be at fault. She couldn't, so someone else had to be. That was that.

"All right, Doc," I said. "I'll remember that."

"Fine," he said, obviously relieved. "Do you think you can find your way home all right tonight? I don't know when I'll be leaving and of course you don't know your hours yet."

I told him I'd be all right by myself; he hurried off. Seething inside, I walked on toward the highway department.

It was on the main floor of the building, and occupied an entire wing. A long counter, facing the entrance door stretched the length of it. A series of cages similar to those in banks fronted on the counter.

It was nine o'clock when I arrived, but no one was there. Finally, at a quarter after nine, an auto-license clerk entered his cage and pointed out Fleming's office to me.

I went down the aisle to a door at the end. It opened into a reception room with an immense executive-type desk and a white-leather upholstered lounge with matching chairs. I knocked on a door marked "Private" and tried the knob. I sat down in one of the chairs and lighted a cigarette.

The nearest ash tray stood by the desk. I'd got up to move it over by me when the door behind me opened and a woman bustled in breathlessly. She was about fifty, trim, sharp-featured.

"What are you doing here?" she demanded. And before I could answer, she had pushed around me and was trying the drawers of the desk.

"Anything missing?" I said.

"What do you want?"

"I was supposed to see Mr. Fleming about a job," I said. "I'm Patrick Cosgrove."

She gave me a tight-lipped smile. "I'm Mr. Fleming's secretary. I don't remember his mentioning your name."

"Senator Burkman spoke to him about it."

"Oh," her face cleared, *"Burkman!* Well, that accounts for it. It probably slipped his mind."

"When will Mr. Fleming be in?" I asked.

"I'm not sure that he can see you when he does come in. Oh, well, drop back in an hour or so if you like. I'll see what I can do."

I thanked her and left, far from happy with the situation. I thought I'd better talk things over with Doc before I went back to Fleming's office, and I went down to the restaurant, hoping to catch him there.

He wasn't there and neither was Burkman. I was on the point of leaving when Hardesty hailed me. He was alone at his table.

"How are you, Pat?" He arose beaming, and shook hands. "Sit right down. Out pretty early, aren't you? Are you by yourself?"

"I didn't think it was early," I said. "But I guess it is. I was looking for Doc."

"He's tied up. Anything I can do?"

"It's about the job I was supposed to have. I thought I had one with the highway department, but I'm not sure now."

"Well, now," he smiled reassuringly. "That won't do at all. Tell me about it."

"Mr. Fleming wasn't in his office, and his secretary practically threw me out. She told me I could come back later, but I got the impression that it wouldn't do me much good."

"Let's see—Burkman was sponsoring you, wasn't he? Hmm, that's not so good."

"You don't think I'll get a job?"

"Oh, yes. You'll get your job. I was just thinking of the matter, uh, objectively." He nodded his head. "Fleming's over there a few tables. We'll tag him when he starts out."

"Thanks very much," I said. "I was getting pretty worried."

"Glad to do it. No trouble at all." He stirred his

coffee, thoughtfully, smiling his warm, confident smile. "Quite a little fracas we had yesterday, eh, Pat?"

"I'm sorry about that," I said. "I'll see that nothing of the kind happens again."

"Oh, I'm not blaming you for it. But I couldn't help feeling a little annoyed with Doc. After all, I did just about as much work on your parole as he did. He should have told you about me beforehand."

"I suppose you're right," I said carefully.

"One serious misstep, something of the kind that happened yesterday, for example, and Doc or no one else could save you from going back to Sandstone. For that matter, Doc himself ..."

"Yes?" I said.

"Oh, well, I probably shouldn't say anything like that."

He might as well have said it: that Doc himself might take a notion to have me returned to prison.

"Why don't you drop up to my office sometime, Pat? I think you and I have a great many things to talk about."

"I'll be glad to come," I said.

"Good!" he smiled. "Well, here comes your man. Fleming! Just a moment."

A tall fat man turned slowly away from a group that was starting for the door, and looked at us sourly. Hardesty took me by the elbow and drew me forward.

"Mr. Fleming, I want you to shake hands with Pat Cosgrove," he said, heartily. "Pat's supposed to go to work in your department, you know."

"Work?" Fleming took the cigar out of his mouth, and barely touched my hand with fat, hard fingers. "Don't you ever look at the calendar, Hardesty?"

Hardesty laughed. "Pat's a good friend of Burkman's. The senator spoke to you about him."

"Burkman's a goddam nuisance," said Fleming, and annoyed remembrance flickered in his small eyes.

"Pat's all set and rarin' to go," said Hardesty jovially. "Would you like to talk to him here or up in your office?"

The fat man grunted. "Office. See Rita." Without another word, he turned and rolled slowly away.

"That's his secretary," Hardesty explained. "Rita Kennedy. Fleming will have called her by the time you get there."

"It's all settled?" I said.

"Sure, she'll fix you up." He slapped me on the back. "I'll have to run, now. Don't forget that other matter."

"I'll remember," I said.

I went back to Fleming's office, not feeling any too sure of myself. But the moment I stepped through the door I knew the job was mine. Rita Kennedy was hardly effusive, but she gave me one of her tight-lipped smiles and motioned for me to draw a chair up to the desk.

"All right, Pat," she said briskly, drawing a heavy manila folder from her desk. "I believe we're all organized, now. Here are your gasoline mileage books, and these are your daily-expense blanks—you're allowed one dollar per meal—and this is your car-requisition card. You know where the state garage is—just two blocks south?"

"Yes, ma'am," I said. "But—"

"Oh, yes. I knew there was something I'd forgotten. Excuse me a moment."

She got up, locked the drawer of the desk, and bustled into the main offices. In a minute or two she was back with a thick stack of mimeographed sheets covered with writing and figures.

"These are the survey forms, Pat. You use one for
each day. You can turn them in, as many as you
complete, every three or four days."

"I see," I nodded. "But what am I supposed to do
with them, Miss Kennedy?"

"Keep your mouth shut and don't leave your car
parked too long in front of beer joints. The newspapers
have given us some awful ridings about stuff of that
kind."

"But ... oh," I said.

"You should kick." She smiled faintly, easing me
toward the door. "Don't forget what I said about the
beer joints."

"I'll remember," I said.

I left the capitol and started south, thinking;
wondering why I should feel ashamed of myself.

A little more than fifteen years before on a day like
this, I'd walked into the First State Bank of Selby and
pointed my sixteen gauge shotgun at the cashier. I
can't tell you why I did it. I only know it wasn't
planned. I'd started for the river to go hunting when I
discovered I only had two shells. And all I'd intended
when I entered the bank was to draw a dollar out of
my savings account.

It was around noon and old Briggs, the cashier, was
by himself. I was carrying my gun because I didn't
want to leave it in my stripped-down Model-T.

Briggs gave me a funny, teasing look and half raised
his hands. And then his hands were going higher, and
his look was frightened; and I was stuttering something
that sounded like, "N-now I'm not—I—I don't mean—
I—I—I won't h-hurt you, Mr. Briggs."

He toppled down to the floor inside the cage, and I
started to run out on the street and call for help.
Instead of that, I scooped up half a dozen packets of

bills and shoved them down inside my sweater, and most of them fell out as I ran out the door.

My car was parked around the corner and Sheriff Nick Nickerson was sitting on the running board. "Been wantin' to see you, boy. Think I got 'er fixed so's you can go to the U next fall." "Gosh," I said, "thanks, Mr. Nickerson." "Writ my nephew up there an' he says you want to make yourself handy around his garage he can swing your board and room an' a little spendin' money." "That's swell," I said. "I can get enough for the tuition and books." "Glad to do it. There ain't nothing around here for a bright young fellow. Seems like the brighter they are the quicker they go to rot." I thanked him again, and got in the car. And then the alarm in the bank began to clatter and he started running and I drove off. Slowly, dazed. Then faster. As fast as I could go.

About a mile out of town, the car begun to sputter and pop and I knew I was almost out of gas. I turned in at the airport and drove across the field.

Frank Miller was spinning the prop of his little old patched-up three seater. It caught and he ran around and crawled inside; and I was out of my car and crawling right in behind him. Judge Lipscomb Lacy was in the passengers' seats; he weighed more than three hundred pounds and he was spread all over both of them. Frank said, "What the hell you think you're doin', Red? Judge Lacy's got 'portant business in the city an'—" "Get goin'." I said. "I'll blast you, Frank. I'll—I'll blast you, I swear to God I will."

I squeezed in, the gun jammed right into Judge Lacy's guts, and I said I'd blast them both, I'd blast him if Frank didn't do what I said and then I'd blast Frank. Judge Lacy's eyes went shut and his face turned green and his head lolled. And Frank said, "All right, you crazy bastard!" And we were in the air. And down again. Bouncing. Rocking from side to side.

"It won't lift us, Red. Honest to Gawd, it won't." "I know," I said. "You want I should dump him out?" "I guess not. He looks awfully sick." "What the hell do you want?" "I don't know."

The door of the plane opened, a long time later it opened, and there was a big crowd out there. And Sheriff Nick Nickerson reached inside and took the gun out of my hands. "Come on now, boy," he said. "You just come along now an' we'll see about this." So I got out, and it was all over. All over except for the trial, with a court-appointed lawyer and Judge Lipscomb Lacy presiding.

... I'd never been ashamed of that. I was not ashamed now. Of that.

The garage manager glanced at my requisition card, and turned me over to a young Negro in overalls. He led me back to the rear, past the motorcycles and the black-and-white trooper cars.

"Yes, sir," he said, stopping. "What kind o' car you like, now?"

"I can have any one I want?" I asked.

"We-ell. Don't believe I'd take none of them big babies. That's a mightly nice little coupe right there. No one's got no call on that."

It was practically new, and a plain unadorned black. Only the license plates identified it as a state car.

"It'll do," I said. "What time do I bring it back in?"

"You live here in town, sir?"

"Yes, I do," I said.

"Well, most of the gen'lemen that lives in town jus' keeps their cars."

"That sounds like a pretty good arrangement," I said.

"Yes, sir," he grinned. "Hardly no one ever kicks on it."

I gave him a dollar tip, put my papers up in back of the seat and drove out.

11

Madeline Flournoy's apartment was on the second floor of a two-story brick building in a semi-residential district. A furniture store occupied the first floor. The upstairs entrance was on a side street, and there were no windows on that side. The blank wall of a warehouse rose on the other side of the street.

There was a door at the head of the stairs and another a few steps up the hallway. I hesitated, then remembered the single mail slot downstairs: both doors were hers. I knocked on the first one.

It opened almost immediately.

"Riding or walking?" She didn't seem surprised to see me. "Where did you park your car?"

"Down the street two blocks on a lot."

"Come on in."

She was wearing a pair of shorts, very short, and a gray wool sweat shirt. Her feet and legs were bare. The long curl of her hair was pulled up on top of her head and fastened with a single pin. The crisp brown end of it stuck out even with her forehead like a little brush.

"Now don't look in there," she said, nodding the brush. And of course I did look in there, into the bedroom with its rumpled bed. "I just got up."

"That Doc," she yawned. "Nothing's too hard for him as long as someone else has to do it."

"Up pretty late?" I said.

"Mmm. Come on. I need coffee!"

"Perhaps I should tell you," I said. "Doc warned me I wasn't to see you."

"Pooey on Doc," she said. "Trust him to order people around. Who the hell is he to tell us what to do?"

"Well," I said. "He's in a pretty good position to tell me what to do."

"Yeah?" She looked at me blankly. "Well, he won't know about it. No one ever comes around here during the day. But no one."

She gave my arm an impatient tug, and I went with her.

There was an areaway to our right almost wholly blocked by a worn plush lounge. She closed the connecting door into the living room, pushed me down on the lounge, and, squeezing past my knees, went into the kitchen.

She came back with two cups of coffee and gave me one. Then she sat down or rather stood on her knees facing me.

"You'd better put your legs up, too," she said. "There's hardly room for them that way."

"This is all right," I said.

"What you squirming for?" She crinkled her eyes. "Have to go to the bathroom? It's right there."

"Thanks, no," I said.

"Now, you look here," she said, shaking the brush of hair. "The door's closed and we've got those other rooms between us and the hallway. And, anyway, no one ever comes up here during the day. Good gosh, if I'd known you were such a scaredy-cat—"

"I thought you knew," I said. "Or I wouldn't have come today. It might make a difference in your wanting to know me."

"Know what? What am I supposed to know?"

"I've just been released from Sandstone," I said. "Doc got my parole for me."

"Oh," she said, softly.

"Fifteen years. Bank robbery."

"I'm awfully sorry, Pat. How old were you?"

"Almost eighteen."

"Almost eighteen," she said. "You didn't hurt anyone, did you?"

"I didn't even get any money," I said, and I told her a little about it, and, oddly enough, I found myself laughing.

She giggled delightedly. She rocked forward on her knees, and burrowed her head against my shoulder.

I put my coffee cup on the floor beside hers and slid my arm around her. She lifted her head and looked at me.

"I've—I've never known anyone quite like you," I said.

"Of course not," she said promptly. "You never will either."

"I'm in a rather peculiar position, Madeline. I can't say and do things I'd like to, that a man normally would."

"Yes," she said. "You are."

"Well—" I was somewhat taken back by her answer, "—we seem to be in agreement."

"I wonder if it had occurred to you that I might be in a pretty peculiar position myself?"

"It had," I said, "and it bothered me a great deal."

"Why?"

"Because I like you. To use an understatement. To

give you a fuller explanation, I'd have to go into the details of what I think are the peculiarities of your position."

"There will now be a brief pause," she said, "while Madame Flournoy goes into a trance and interprets Professor Cosgrove's message."

"I think you know what I mean," I said.

"Quiet," she said. And, turning, she lay down and put her head in my lap.

I bent my head and kissed her. She gave me two quick kisses in return before moving her mouth away. There was something about them, something so warm and confiding and innocent, that I wanted to thrust my hands into my pockets and keep them there; to sit on them, if necessary. And, of course, I didn't.

She opened her eyes and looked up at me. She raised one small finger and put it on my lip and moved it up and down. She lowered the hand and let it lie on mine.

"What are you doing in—in all this anyway?" I said.

"What are you?"

"That's hardly the same thing."

"Isn't it?" she said. "You did an impulsive, seemingly easy thing—something that seemed to promise a lot— when you were too young to judge the consequences. So did I."

I lighted a cigarette, tossing the match into my saucer. She pursed her lips and crinkled her eyes at me, and I lowered the cigarette while she took a long deep puff.

"Well?" she said, puffing the smoke out in rings.

"It's hard for me to imagine," I said, "that you'd put up with anything over any very long period that you didn't want to."

"You put up with Sandstone, didn't you?"

She took another puff from my cigarette, and bobbed her head emphatically. "When I first saw you on the capitol steps yesterday—oh, yes, I did *see* you— I thought, there, that's it—"

"I thought the same thing."

"I know you did, honey." She patted my cheek. "And I made up my mind to bump into you on the way back, or—or drop something, or fall down in front of you. Anything to get to know you. And then I found you were with Doc and it made me kind of sick inside. But still ..."

"I know," I said.

"You must have had some pretty strong friends to set Doc in motion. If they could get him to swing the parole they can probably get him to put through a pardon ... Did I say something wrong?"

"I don't have any friends," I said. "Doc got me out on his own."

"Huh?" She gestured with her hand. "You mean just like that?"

"Just like that." I told her about the letter I'd written him. "I'd never seen him before."

"But, why? Pat! You didn't agree to—you didn't promise—"

"What could I promise?" I said.

"But—"

"I know," I said. "There's a reason. But the only one I can think of doesn't make sense. That I'm valuable or will be valuable to him just by being what I am. That he thinks I will be."

"Thinks?"

"It's just a hunch," I nodded. "He had a reason for getting me out; someone else had another. His plan isn't going to come off ... and the other will."

"Now, that *doesn't* make sense," she said. "Believe

me, Pat, that guy knows what he's doing. Always. I've worked for him for years, and I've been on the inside of every crooked deal he's pulled. I—I—"

"Don't feel bad about it," I said. "For a person who hasn't had to work at it to stay alive, you're pretty good."

"What . . . I don't understand."

"Lying. Pretending. You're Doc's right hand. You knew that he was getting me out of Sandstone. You know why he got me out. Why don't you tell me? What has he got on you that makes you afraid to talk?"

"Is that why you came here today, Pat, to pump me?"

"I didn't think I'd have to pump you. I thought you had some of the same feeling for me that I have for you. I—"

"Oh, I do, Pat!" She thrust herself upwards and clung to me tightly. "You must believe me, honey. I do feel that way!"

"Tell me, then."

"Don't—don't let him make you do anything, Pat! Talk to me first! Don't do anything without talking to me. Will you promise that?"

"I—" My scalp crawled suddenly. "Did you lock that hall door?"

"I probably didn't. No one ever comes up here during the day."

"Someone did," I said, and I nodded at the glass panel of the connecting door.

Just as he looked through it, grinning.

12

He was about my height, though heavier; and he had a lipless tobacco-stained mouth and little red-rimmed pig eyes and a nose that might have been made out of soiled putty. He wore a blue serge suit, without a vest, a snap-brimmed gray hat, and black high-topped shoes. Shoes and hat were spotless. The suit wasn't.

I knew what he was before he ever spit the toothpick out of his mouth and showed his credentials.

I nodded and handed them back to him.

"This gentleman is with the probation department, Madeline," I said. "He's caught me in a pretty serious violation of my parole."

"Huh!" She stared at him fiercely. "That doesn't give him a license to housebreak! Where's your warrant, you—"

"You don't understand, Madeline. This gentleman can have me sent back to Sandstone. Now just close the door, and lock it this time. We don't want to be disturbed while we're talking, do we, sir?"

He grinned and the caution in his pig eyes disappeared.

"Now," I said, smiling, staring straight into his eyes. "What did you have in mind, sir? How would a couple of C-notes do?"

"Two C's?" His ugly face lit up, then contorted into a scowl. "Huh-uh. Ain't half enough. Make it five."

"Would that be enough?"

"I said so, didn't I? For five it's a deal."

"You're making a mistake," I said. "It's worth much more than five hundred for me to stay out of Sandstone. I'm afraid I can't tell you how much it is worth to me. I'd have to show you. Now, don't be alarmed, sir ..."

He was alarmed, or beginning to be. But I was smiling, and holding his eyes; and so he stood and watched while I slid out of my coat and shirt and undershirt.

I heard Madeline gasp.

He gulped and whistled softly. "My God!" he whispered.

"You were looking at those welts, sir?" I said. "Why they were nothing, relatively speaking. A little annoying, perhaps, when you get them full of gnats and salt sweat and rock dust; but nothing compared to those ribs. You should have seen them popping out through the flesh like splinters bursting through tree bark. You should have seen this arm the day a friend tried to chop it off for me. That's right, sir. A friend. He got thirty days in the hole and I got three weeks in the hospital.

"I hope I didn't upset you, sir?" I said. "I just wanted to demonstrate that I don't and won't have enough to pay you to stay out of Sandstone. Which brings us to our problem. Since I can't pay you, what can I do to show how highly I value your silence? What can I give you ... that will last and always be enough? That you'll never want any more of?"

He took a step backwards.

"B-better watch out now, Red," his voice cracked

and rose. "B-better watch out, k-keep away from me! Ain't n-no h-harm done. J-just a joke, n-no h-harm in j-jokin' ..."

He stumbled and tried to throw his hands in front of his face.

I chopped down and in, with the edge of my hands, getting both kidneys at once. His arms came down and I cuffed him, spinning him around. I jerked his tie tight, as tight as I could get it, took a turn around his neck with each end, and knotted it in the back.

I let him drop to the floor and watched him thrash about, scratching and clawing at his throat.

As from a distance I heard Madeline say, "He'll d-die, Pat. Don't let him die ..."

"A few oranges," I said, "in a net bag. Or a flour sack. And something to cut the tie."

"What do you want with the oranges?"

"You'd better hurry," I said, and I kicked him away as he tried to crawl up my legs.

She came running back with a paring knife, and four or five oranges in the bottom of a red net bag.

I swung the sack with both hands. It struck him in the chest and flattened him. It frightened him to the last degree he could be frightened. I beat him all over the chest and stomach and thighs, and then I turned him over and beat him up and down the back.

I jerked him upright, cut the necktie and tossed him into a chair. He sat there panting, pawing at his throat, his eyes rolling up and down in his head.

I had Madeline bring me a washrag and a comb, and I sponged off his face and combed his hair for him. I set his hat back on his head, and buttoned up his coat.

"Do you understand?" I said. "That's what it means."

"I—" he nodded his head. "I g-get you."

"You might not make a charge stick," I said. "And if you did, I'd still find a way of seeing you. I can't lose any more, and you can lose and keep losing. So I'd see you. Once. I wouldn't have to see you after that."

I jerked a thumb toward the door. "You've got it. Keep it."

He wasn't hurt. No one who was hurt could have got out of there that fast. I laughed a little as the door slammed.

Madeline grinned, a slow fixed grin.

"You see I didn't kill him," I said. "I didn't even hurt him."

"What about the—way—?"

"The oranges? That's the old dummy-chucker's trick. You know, the fake-accident racket."

"I guess I don't know, Pat," she said slowly, "much of anything."

"A man's supposed to have been in an accident, but he doesn't have any marks on him. So a confederate takes a bag of oranges and beats him with them. They don't hurt him, but they turn him black and blue. He's a mass of bruises."

"Oh."

"Our friend struck me as being unusually susceptible to fear. He'll probably believe to his dying day that he barely escaped being killed."

"And he didn't, did he?"

I thought I had explained. "No," I said, shortly. "Not that time."

I picked up my undershirt and put it on. I put on my shirt and tie. I reached for my coat, but she was ahead of me. She held it for me, pushing it up onto my shoulders; and then she slid around in front, holding me tight around the waist.

"I understand, Pat. Oh, I do understand, honey!"

"I guess," I said. "You understand too much."

"It's all right, Pat. I don't blame you. But—Oh, let's just forget it!"

"I made you afraid," I said, "with what I did to that guy. You're afraid I'll do the same thing to Doc. What's Doc to you, Madeline? What is he planning that makes you think I might try to kill him if I found it out?"

She shook her head, stubbornly. "There's nothing I can tell you, Pat," she said. "Nothing. If you love me, you'll have to believe that."

"All right," I said.

She gave me a final squeeze. "Betcha everything's going to be all right," she declared, brightly. "Betcha it will."

"Betcha," I said.

I knew she was crying the second the door closed behind me.

13

Hardesty had a suite of offices on the top floor of the city's tallest skyscraper. The legend on the series of doors leading to the reception room read:

Hardesty & Hardesty
Attorneys at Law

and the receptionist, a querulous elderly woman with a suspicious stare, presided over a room as old fashioned as the building was new.

I put my cigarette out, and folded my hands. After some fifteen minutes, Hardesty came out of his office.

He nodded to me, tossing some papers on the receptionist's desk.

"I'll be tied up the rest of the morning, Mrs. Smithson," he told her. "Just make a note of any calls I have, will you?"

"Tied up!" she exclaimed. "You're supposed to be in court at eleven o'clock."

"Clark will handle it; nothing important," he said. "Come right on in, Pat."

He closed the door on her disapproving grunt, an abashed smile on his darkly handsome face. "Friendly little thing, isn't she?"

"An old employee?" I said.

"One of my grandfather's." He put a match to his

cigarette and held it for mine. "He and my father were partners, in case you're wondering about the firm name."

"That must make it one of the oldest law firms in the state."

"I think it is," he nodded. "Quite an outfit, eh? When my father died, I planned on fancying things up a bit but you can see how far I got. I imagine if the other building we were in hadn't been condemned I wouldn't even have got us moved over here. Anyhow, stodginess is an asset with the kind of clientele we have."

"Yes," I said. "I suppose it would be."

"Not quite what you expected, huh?" He gave me a shrewd glance. "You didn't think an old and respectable law firm would be mixed up with a guy like Doc."

"Frankly, no," I said. "Although I'm not being critical of Doc."

"Mmm. Of course not. Well, confidentially, Pat; I'm not involved with Doc a bit more than I can help. You know how it is. You want to swing a piece of business with the state, and the first thing you know you find Doc or someone like him in your path. And you either work with him or you don't put your deal across."

I nodded noncommittally. The less I had to say about Doc, I felt, the better.

"Let's see, now. How long have you been out of Sandstone?"

"Almost three weeks."

"And you're pretty badly worried. Oh, don't be afraid to say so, Pat."

"All right," I said. "But it's a pretty hard thing to put into words. The trouble is—is Mrs. Luther. She won't leave me alone."

"Oh?"

"She came back to my room the second night I was there, and she almost got me in very serious trouble with Doc. She's followed the same line of conduct ever since. She does things that, well, look like hell."

"Mmm," murmured Hardesty. "That's embarrassing, all right, but I wouldn't be too disturbed about it. Doc won't blame you for it."

"He shouldn't," I said. "But he does. I can't tell him it isn't my fault. I can't brush her off. I can't let her go on. Whatever I do or don't do, I have Doc angry with me. I'm afraid it might lead to my parole being canceled."

"Umm. And if you thought it was going to be, you'd try to make a run for it. Well, we can't have that; can't have that, at all."

"I wonder if you'd have enough influence with her to make her stop," I said.

"We-ell—" he pursed his lips, "—yes. Yes. I can do that little thing for you."

"I'll appreciate it very much," I said.

"That isn't all you're worried about, Pat."

"No," I said.

"Just no? You've trusted me with this other matter."

"I think you must know," I said. "I can't help wondering why Doc got me out of Sandstone."

"You can't feature Doc doing that unless he stood to cash in on it?"

"I didn't say that," I said. "I do feel it strange that he did it at this particular time. Judging by the way Burkman was treated and some other things I've seen and heard, Doc's crowd may lose out at the election. They need everything they've got for themselves. Why should they use up a lot of their steam in helping me?"

"A good question, Pat. But the answer is simple

enough. Ever hear of Fanning Arnholt, president of the National Phalanx?"

"The big patriotic organization?"

"The super-patriotic organization," Hardesty corrected. "What Arnholt and the Phalanx says, we common mortals feel obliged to heed and obey."

"Yes?" I said.

"Arnholt's slated to make six speeches in this state, the first here in the capital about two weeks from today. He's going to attack a number of the textbooks now in use on the grounds that they're subversive. When he does, it's going to be an easy matter to get those texts thrown out and a new line adopted."

"I see," I said. "But—"

"I know. You're wondering why we fool with books when we've got the oil crowd to play with. But we— Doc's gang *does* get to the oil companies. A big stink about textbooks diverts the public's attention from them. It's worth heavy dough to them to get that attention diverted. We take a double rack-off."

He grinned and spread his hands, watching me out of warm dark eyes. "A dirty business all the way around, Pat, but with a boob crop like we've got here you just naturally find a threshing crew. And it's worked out to your advantage. Doc set this deal up and agreed to cut his associates in on it. In return for that, they put through your parole."

"But that still doesn't answer my question," I said. "Why did Doc want me paroled?"

"Well," he hesitated. "I'm not sure that I can help you there."

"You must know," I said. "You have a great deal more to lose than Burkman and the others. You wouldn't have taken a hand in this unless you knew exactly where it was leading."

"You mean, unless I was certain of getting as much as Doc?" He shook his head. "Maybe not, Pat. There are other things besides money."

"You're putting words in my mouth," I said. "My point is that you know why Doc wanted me out of Sandstone."

"I might. But why should I tell you?"

"Well ..." I was stumped by the flatness of the question. "I can't give you anything for the information. But you indicated that you were my friend, that I could trust you ..."

"Did you believe me?"

"Well ..."

"Well, you see how it is, Pat," he said, grinning engagingly. "You're asking for something that you won't give. And, as you pointed out a moment ago, I have a great deal to lose. Tell me. Don't you have any ideas of your own?"

"None at all. There's nothing I can do for anyone. I don't have anything, that I can see, but a bad reputation."

"Very bad," he nodded.

"You mean that's something in itself?"

"Let's just say it's something for you to think about."

"But I don't see how—"

"Go on, Pat. You're doing fine."

"Then there's Mrs. Luther," I said. "If she got Doc sore enough at me to have my parole canceled, his plan, whatever it is, would fall through. I'd be right back where I started and all his time and effort would be wasted. Of course, I know he's unreasonable about her, but—"

"Think, Pat. Can't you think of a set of circumstances where it might be profitable to anyone for you to be returned to Sandstone?"

I stared at him blankly. He nodded, narrow-eyed.

"I can see that you can't," he said. "But you will. You'll see that and the other angle, as well. When you do, when you begin to get an inkling of their significance, we'll have a talk."

"Thanks," I said, and I shook hands limply.

"You'll be all right for the time being. There's this Arnholt matter. Nothing's going to happen until that's wound up."

"I'm glad to know that," I said.

"You can depend on it. Meanwhile, I'll see what I can do about getting Mrs. Luther off your neck. She's rather fond of me, you know."

He winked and poked me in the ribs. I let him lead me out the hall door of his office.

"I trust our little talk will remain confidential," he said, as he shook hands with me again.

He gave me a final smile and nod, and very gently closed the door.

14

Suddenly everything was all right again. As right as it had been in the beginning. I didn't have to avoid Lila Luther; she made a point of keeping out of my way. And on those rare occasions when we did encounter each other she was barely polite.

Almost overnight the constraint which I had seen building up in Doc disappeared. He became the old Doc, alternately slangy and grammatical, flippant and profound; generous, good natured: a man who made the best of a shabby situation.

I got paid the week following my visit to Hardesty, on Friday, as I remember. I hadn't worked a full month, but I was paid for one.

I gave the check to Doc to cash for me, and he brought the money back to my room the next night. Smiling, he refused to take a cent of it.

"Just hang onto your money, Pat," he said. "You won't want to stick in one of those political jobs always, and you probably won't be able to, anyway. Hang onto it, and you'll have something to operate on when your parole runs out."

"I wonder if I should start a bank account?" I said.

"That's a good idea," he said. "We'll do that some day soon when I can spare the time to go down and introduce you."

I left the house every morning at a reasonably early hour, and never returned before five in the afternoon. Usually I spent an hour or so at Madeline's. The rest of the time I saw picture shows or read in the public library or drove around.

One morning, a few days after payday, I drove out to the place where Doc and I had stopped my first night out of Sandstone: the place where the sludge from the oil wells had widened the river into an expanse of stinking and treacherous mud. I don't think I sought the spot consciously; it was no attraction which would justify a drive of ten or twelve miles. But I found myself there suddenly, and I pulled the car off the road and walked up to the stone bench. I sat down on it, and leaned forward, carefully. I scooped up a handful of pebbles and began dropping them down into the mud.

Now and then I caught the faint, dull clatter of pipe tongs, or the muted *"Deee-ropp itt!"* of some faraway roughneck. And the bank after bank of quadruple boilers belched lazy smoke into the air. And even here, where I was, there was a rhythmic tremble to the earth, a constant shivering as the mud-hog pumps growled and spat out their burden.

I took a long, deep breath and slowly let it out again. It was good to be here, here or any place that wasn't Sandstone. Every day I realized a little more how good it was. To be able to be off guard; to smile or laugh when you wanted to; just to breathe—easily; to think instead of scheme.

I leaned forward and smiled down into the black surface below; and back came another smile, my reflection, thoughtful but reassuring.

Hang on to yourself, Red. Hang on, or—
A hand came down on my shoulder.

"Better hang on to the bench, Red. You might fall in."

In one unthinking instant, I had lowered my shoulders, caught the arm and shifted my weight forward and upward. Luckily she yelled, and a reflex action set in against the first one. Otherwise, Myrtle Briscoe would have gone into the river instead of down on to the bench. And I, the chances are, would have gone with her with a bullet through my head.

There was a highway patrol car parked near mine, and a state trooper was bounding up the slope, tugging at his holstered .45.

He almost had it out when Myrtle Briscoe leaped up from the bench and waved her arms at him.

"Hold it, Tony!" she gasped. Then she got her breath and yelled, "Dammit to hell, hold it!"

The trooper paused. "You sure you're all right, Miss Briscoe?"

"Hell yes!" She let out a snort of laughter, and made brushing motions at her clothes. "Shook up but all together."

The trooper looked from me to her, an expression of sullen disappointment on his swarthy face. "You sure you don't want me to—"

"I want you to go back to the car and sit there!"

He turned and went back. Myrtle sat down, shaking her head.

"Don't know why it is," she said. "Give a guy a gun and he can't wait to use it."

"I've noticed that," I said, sitting down at her side. "I'm sorry if I startled you, Miss Briscoe."

"Oh, well. One good startle deserves another. What are you doing so far from town, Red?"

"I didn't think it was far."

"Aren't you working?"

"I still have my job," I said. "I'm caught up for a few hours."

"Okay," she said. "Now let me tell you something, Red. Tony and I gave you a long tail all the way from town. About an hour ago we lost you. We go on down the road about twenty miles and then we come back, and here you are. How do you explain that?"

"You mean I was trying to shake you?" I said. "I didn't even know you were following me."

"How come we didn't see you or at least your car?"

"That's simple. For one thing, there were probably other cars between yours and mine. Mainly, however, you didn't want to see me. You wanted to believe I was skipping out. You were so certain I was going to that you probably wouldn't have seen me if I'd waved a red flag at you."

"Now, look, Red. You know doggone well what I'm talking about. What about that car?"

"It belongs to the state. You know that, Miss Briscoe."

Her mouth dropped open and her eyes flashed. She jerked a paper from the pocket of her old-fashioned skirt, and thrust it at me.

It was one of those small legal papers which list title transfers and mortgages and similar information. Myrtle Brisco put her fingers on a red-circled item under Automobile Transfer:

> *Capital Car Co. to Patrick M. Cosgrove*
> *'42 Fd. Cp., $175*

"I suppose it's another Cosgrove," said Myrtle, sarcastically. "Go on, tell me it is."

I shook my head. I didn't know what it was all about, but I knew it wouldn't be another Cosgrove. It was all done too neatly.

I'd drawn a check for $250. After allowing for a month's expenses, I'd have a surplus of just about $175 to spend on a car. I hadn't done it, but I wouldn't dare tell Myrtle that. She'd never liked the idea of my being paroled to Doc. If she got the idea that he was using me, that there was something seriously wrong...

I was in a trap, and I couldn't go out by the door. That led back to Sandstone. I had to stay in until I found my own exit.

"I'm sorry," I said. "I didn't know it was a violation of my parole."

"Who said it was? What I want to know is why you bought it? That title was transferred yesterday, but the car was still on the sales lot this morning."

"I thought I'd pick it up over the week end," I said.

"But why did you buy it—a jalopy like that—when the state lets you have a first class car for nothing?"

"It's simple enough," I said. "Since I don't need it for myself, I obviously intend to resell it. I'm pretty handy with tools. I can fix it up in my spare time and make a little money on it."

"Well ..." She stared at me suspiciously.

"That's what I intend to do, Miss Briscoe."

"Now," she nodded. "That's what you intend to do *now*. What did you—did you honest-to-God buy that car, Red?"

"I don't understand."

"I don't either. But let it go. Get that car off the lot today. And don't lose any time about re-selling it."

"Yes, ma'am," I said. "Do you want me to drive back to town ahead of you?"

"That won't be necessary," she snapped. And then her voice and her face softened. "I'm trying to help you, Red, and that's all I am trying to do. Why don't you give me a chance?"

"Yes, ma'am?"

"Come out of it! For God's sake come out of your shell before you rot in it." She put a hand on my knee and leaned toward me. "I'm sure you're in a jam, a damned bad one. Tell me about it."

"There's nothing I can tell you," I said.

"There. You see? You don't even have to think any more; you slide off center automatically. Doc's got you mixed up in something, and you don't know how to get out of it, hasn't he?"

"Why should Doc do that?"

"Red—!" She sighed and removed her hand. "Suppose I said this to you. Suppose I told you I knew you were on the level and wanted to stay that way and any trouble you were in wasn't your own fault."

"There's nothing to tell at the moment," I said carefully. "But something might come up ..."

"Yes, Red?"

"I understand you always keep your word," I said. "You always make good on a threat or a promise. So make that supposition of yours a little more specific, and I'll believe you. Tell me you'll trust me to do what I have to, what I think is right, and that you'll keep me from going back to Sandstone."

"Well," she laughed, irritatedly, "that's a pretty big load to buy blind, Red."

I nodded. "But no bigger than the one you're asking me to buy."

"Yes, it is. You see, Red, there's such a hell of a lot more involved than just you and me. For almost ten years, now, Doc's crowd has been riding high and handsome. This time, in this coming election, it looks like they're going to lose out. They're getting desperate. They're looking for some way to discredit me. You could be it."

"I don't see how I could be used," I said. "Anyway,

I've been given to understand that you can stay in office as long as you want to."

"I've stayed in for thirty years, but that doesn't mean I can keep on doing it. And when I go, whatever small reform element there is goes with me. A first-class scandal will put any office-holder in the street— and the straighter he's been the harder it'll hit him. He'll either lose out entirely or he'll have to do so much horse-trading that he won't be able to do anything in his job."

"But—"

"Yeah, I know. I didn't sign your parole. But I did consent to it, and you're my obligation. Let you get in a really bad scrape, and it'll come back on me. Let me get it in the neck, and the whole reform slate will collapse. That automatically leaves Doc's crowd in the saddle. This is a one-party state. The people don't vote for candidates, they vote against them."

"I understand," I said. "But how am I going to be used to discredit you?"

"I don't know, Red. But I can think of any number of things you could do that would pull the trick. That's why I want you to level with me. And I'll go along with you as far as I can, Red. That's a promise."

She stood up tiredly and began brushing at her perpetually wrinkled skirt. The sun was full out by now, and it etched every line of her harsh, haggard face. Her faded topknot of hair was more gray than red.

I stood up also, and she looked up into my face for a moment, squinting her eyes against the sun. Then she took hold of my arm, pushed me gently aside and strode past me and down the hill.

Watching her, watching the firm unfaltering stride, I somehow felt ashamed; and I wanted to run after her or call her back. And I stayed where I was and kept my mouth closed.

I knew I was making a mistake, just how bad a one I was yet to discover. But I knew of nothing else to do.

15

The Capital Car Company had a block-long sales lot on the outskirts of the downtown business district. A salesman directed me to a small frame office, surrounded and almost hidden by cars. I introduced myself to the manager, a brisk gold-toothed little man named Rivers.

"Oh, sure," he said instantly. "Wife bought it for you. Very fine lady, very fine. Want to take a look at it?"

"I thought I'd take it with me," I said.

"Take it or leave it. Wife said you might want to leave it a while. A fine lady, that."

"Fine," I said.

He led me halfway down a row of automobiles and stopped before a Ford coupe. It wasn't junk, by any means, despite the scratched and lustreless body. The tires were new. I lifted the hood and saw an engine as clean as though it had been scrubbed with soap and water.

"Gettin' a buy there," Rivers declared. "Why, I bet you I coulda got two, two and a quarter for that car this morning if I hadn't already sold it. Little old lady was down here lookin' at it. Tell she knew cars, too."

A Negro youth, an employee of the company, drove

the car out to Doc's house for me. Rivers followed in another car to take the youth back to town.

I left the coupe and the state car at the curb, and went up the walk to the house. As I climbed the steps the venetian blind at one of the front windows moved, and when I opened the front doors Mrs. Luther was standing in the door of her apartment.

She was wearing a flowered silk house coat with a bodice of some very sheer material. She smiled and stood back from the door, inviting me in.

"Now aren't you a bad man!" she cried. "You found out about our surprise."

"Is Doc here?" I said.

"Oh, no. He's gone for the day. Come in."

I stepped inside, stopping as near the door as I could without standing close to her. She closed the door, gave me another bright chiding smile and led me to one of the over-stuffed lounges.

"Now," she said, pushing me down on the lounge with a playful gesture. "How did you find out?"

"Wasn't I supposed to?" I said.

"Of course not. Not yet."

"Oh—" I hesitated, "well, you can probably guess, Mrs. Luther. The highway department gets a daily list of title transfers. I saw that I owned a car, so I went down and got it. Shouldn't I have?"

"Well ... as long as you did. Of course, we intended to give it to you on your birthday."

"That was very nice of you," I said, "but I wonder if you haven't made a mistake? My birthday was in March, more than two months ago."

"Oh, *no!*" she said. "Why, Doctor thought it was in May!"

"That's too bad. If you or Doc want to get your money back ..."

She shook her head, doubtfully. She was sure Doc wouldn't want to do that. I murmured more thanks, wondering what went on beneath that vapidly beautiful face.

May and March. The months could easily have been confused. And the present of a car wasn't at all out of keeping with Doc's other acts of generosity toward me. I didn't need one, immediately, but circumstances might change to where I would. What actually was there to be suspicious about?

I looked up at Lila Luther suddenly and caught a peculiar expression in her eyes. Something that was a mixture of shame and hunger. I smiled at her, and she smiled back; shyly, a faint blush spreading across the tawny cheeks. She felt the blush, too, and tried to fix her face against it.

I put out my hand, and let the fingers trail across her breasts.

She gasped, but she didn't pull away. She sat and waited, biting at her lip.

"You're out of character, Mrs. Luther," I said. "Or are you in character? It's got to be one way or the other."

"I—I don't know what you mean." I could feel her mind racing, trying to think and not to think at the same time. "Y-you've got no right to question me!"

"You made one pass at me after another," I said, "and you weren't particular where or when you made them. And then Hardesty told you to lay off, and you did. You didn't count on my making the passes. You don't know what to do, now that I have."

"I—" her eyes were glazing. "I know what to do."

"Spill it! You were told to begin. You were told to stop. What's it all about?"

She didn't answer. She wriggled, moving closer to

me; and her lips parted, and her eyelids flickered lazily. She seemed to have taken a deep, swelling breath and held it.

It was a good act, if it was one. I decided to see if it was, and, if so, how good. I caught the bodice with both hands and pulled out and down.

It came apart like paper, and she fell against me, flinging her arms around me, and crying.

"P-Pat!" It was almost a sob, frantic, hysterical with passion. "Oh, Pat ..."

I let her draw me forward and down.

We still lay together, but I was thinking. The ash-blonde hair was sweetly damp against my face, and her lips brushed my ear, kissing, whispering, and the soft ripe body began to move again in tentative rhythm.

But I was thinking.

What if Doc should come in, now, I thought. What if the door should open and ...

The door did open.

A silver-backed hair brush stood on edge on the coffee table, mirroring the opening door. Mirroring Doc.

And, then, as gently as it had opened it closed again.

It closed; and cautiously the screen door opened and closed.

Seconds later I heard the quiet purr of a distant motor. Distant, then more distant.

Doc, the insanely jealous, had seen this—*this!*—and driven away.

It all had taken place in seconds, not more than a minute. Too swiftly for shock and fear to follow. And Lila Luther hadn't seen or heard.

I sat up. Shock was gripping me at last. A cold, weak

feeling spread up through my chest and throat, and cold sweat broke out on my forehead.

"Darling!" She sat up, also, anxiety and hunger blending on her face. "What's the matter?"

"I don't know," I said. "Felt sick, all of a sudden."

She whispered, "Maybe you'd better go," and I went.

I wanted to tell her, to explain, and reason that had become unreason held me silent. Perhaps she shouldn't know. Perhaps it would precipitate a crisis if she did. Why and how I didn't know, but I sensed the danger. She couldn't be trusted. She'd lied about the car. She'd lied figuratively, ever since I'd come to this house. She knew what was going on, and I didn't, and if I told her this ...

I didn't know. I didn't know what might happen. But I wasn't going to tell her and find out.

16

The sign on the pebble-glassed door read:

E.A. Eggleston

Investigations

The office was in an old five-story building down near the public market.

He couldn't be too good, I'd thought, being in that location. He didn't have to be good, to know what I wanted to, and I didn't want anyone that would be really sharp, that would get ideas and follow them up.

He was tall, and thin-faced and drowsy looking. His scuffed crepe-soled shoes were up on his desk when I went in, and his big bony hands were folded across his stomach. A crumpled gray hat was pulled low on his forehead.

He didn't shift the hat or his position during the half hour or so that I was there.

"Cosgrove," he said in a soft, deep voice. "What do you do, Cosgrove?"

"Do you have to know that?" I said.

"Got to know whether you're worth killing. Whether you're in a business, say, which would suffer from your permanent absence."

"I'm not."

"Heavy on the cuff to anyone? Anyone out real dough if you kick off?"

"No."

"No dependent nor close relatives? No wife?"

"No."

"But you think you may have been insured without your knowledge?"

"I—yes."

"Why?"

"Well, I don't actually think that I am," I said. "I just thought that I might be."

He didn't say anything for a minute or more. Finally, when I was beginning to think he'd dozed off, he spoke:

"Went to a dentist one time to get a tooth pulled. Knew the one that needed pulling would hurt like hell, so I pointed out another one to him. Looks like you're about as smart as I was."

I laughed. "I'm not deliberately lying to you, Eggleston. There are people who would be hurt pretty badly if they knew I'd made an inquiry like this. I can't let them know that I have."

"So?"

"About a month ago a certain party did me a very expensive favor. Since then I've received several others. I'd never met this party before, and I can't think of any way I could provide a return on the investment. Unless I've been insured."

"Ask this party why he or she had done said favors?"

"Not a straight question. The implication was that they were pure philanthropy. That doesn't fit in with what I know about this party."

He sat motionless, silent, staring down at his hands.

"I thought there might be some sort of underwriters' bureau that could give you the information," I said. "Without, of course, letting this party know that I'd asked."

"Um," he said. "It'll cost you twenty dollars, Mr. Cosgrove."

"That's reasonable," I said, and I took out a twenty and laid it on the desk.

He lifted a foot slightly and dragged the bill under his heel.

"You're not insured, Mr. Cosgrove. Anything else?"

"Now, look," I said. "I paid for certain information—"

"Which you received, on very good authority. I've done a great deal of insurance work. No one has taken out a policy on you—providing you've told me the truth."

"I've told it, but—"

"For one party to insure another, he must have what is known as an insurable interest. He must present reasonably good evidence that he has little or nothing more to gain by the insured's demise than he has by his continued existence. The insured's death must represent a sentimental loss, as in the case of husband and wife, a monetary one, or both. No one, it would appear, has an insurable interest in you ..."

Apparently he had little to do but sleep, and insurance was a hobby of his. He continued to talk for almost fifteen minutes, scarcely moving or altering the deep, soft monotone; covering every phase of the business that might possibly concern me.

At last he stopped, and I stood up.

"By the way, Mr. Cosgrove ..."

"Yes?"

"Anyone with the education which you ostensibly have should have known he wasn't insured. Anyone who gets around at all would know it."

"Maybe I don't get around very much," I said.

"My own thought."

"From what I knew," I said, "I was pretty sure I wasn't insured, but I thought things might have changed recently."

"Not that recently, Mr. Cosgrove. You're still a young man. You couldn't have been out of circulation very long."

"Good-bye," I said.

"Known the party about a month," he droned. "Did you a very great favor. And you're suspicious. Why don't you remove yourself from this party's vicinity? From the state, for that matter?"

I stopped and turned. He nodded drowsily.

"You can't leave, can you? So. Yes. You can't leave. I'm beginning to think you might have excellent grounds for your suspicions. Another twenty, please?"

I went back to the desk and laid a second bill on it. He raked it under his heel.

"How long were you in, Mr. Cosgrove?"

"Fifteen years of ten to life."

"And you were unacquainted with the party who got your parole—bought it, shall we say?"

"That's right."

"So are you, Mr. Cosgrove. You have good reason for alarm. A pardon could have been obtained as cheaply and easily. With a pardon you could have gone away—far out of your benefactor's periphery. He is not a philanthropist."

"Good-bye," I said.

"So."

He nodded and seemed to fall asleep, and I left.

More information ... which I didn't know how to use.

17

One of the worst things that prison does to a man is imbue him with the feeling that he is always in the wrong: that others may rightfully do what they will with him, while the things he does, through error or otherwise, are wholly inexcusable.

I felt that way about Doc, about the way he had seen Lila and me. I was certain by now that I was being forced to work against myself. I was sure that I owed him nothing, apologies included. Still, I did feel guilty. I did, and I couldn't help it.

I stayed away from the house until almost midnight that night, and got away early the next morning. By the evening of that day, some of my sense of guilt had worn off. I was still uneasy but I hoped, if he noticed the fact, he would attribute it to the business over the car.

I brought the subject up as soon as he stepped inside my room.

"Mmm," he nodded, thoughtfully. "I should have known that Myrtle would read the legal papers."

"I appreciate it just the same," I said.

"Don't mention it, Pat. We'll try to do better next year."

He left after a quick drink with me. I flopped down

on the bed, relieved, and hating myself for being relieved.

Willie came in to remove my dinner dishes, and I tried to tell myself that it was he, and not Doc, who had looked in on Lila and me. He would have been in the house while Doc would have had no reason to be there.

But I knew better than that. It had been Doc. He'd expected me to come there, because of the car. Probably he'd followed me from the sales lot. And when he'd seen Lila and me ...

Why hadn't he reacted as he should, as the insanely jealous Doc I knew would have? Did he intend to settle with me later, when I was least expecting it? Or had he held off for purely practical reasons—because a blow-up would spoil the plan in which I played a part?

It could be either way or both. And it could be—I sat up on the bed, suddenly—*it could be that Doc actually didn't care about his wife; that the jealousy was all an act!*

I got up and paced the floor, excited, almost seeing the answer to the riddle.

It *had* been an act! Looking back now I could see the falsity of it; how badly it had been overplayed. Doc showing up, always at the most embarrassing moment. Lila haughtily dramatic, taunting him. Throwing whiskey in his face.

It had been rotten acting, but I had been taken in by it. I had been so impressed that I was afraid Doc might drop my parole. I'd told Hardesty that, hinted that I might skip out, and immediately the funny business had stopped. They didn't want me to leave. They'd wanted only to build Doc up in my mind as a certain type of person.

It all added up. Hardesty had told Doc how I felt, and

Doc had told Lila to leave me alone. He'd followed me to the house the day before to reassure me in case Lila fell down on the job. And when he saw Lila apparently was doing more than all right he'd gone quietly away again.

But what about Hardesty? Why, when he so obviously distrusted and detested Doc, had he told him of my visit? He wanted me to share his distrust and hatred. He meant to work me up to the point where I would. That was my answer: I was not yet, in his opinion, sufficiently worked up. I was not ready to be used. Until I was, he was chiefly interested in seeing that I did nothing which might cause me to be returned to Sandstone.

Myrtle Briscoe—I stopped in my pacing and sat down again. Myrtle. She was using me to get Doc. I was a rope she was giving him with which to hang himself.

And Doc . . . Doc had foreseen that she would know, and guessed that she would react as she had. He was tolling out rope of his own. He was certain he could tighten it before she could tighten hers.

And Mrs. Luther? Was she working with one of the three or did she, too, have a plan?

And Madeline . . . ?

No, not Madeline. I'd never had the slightest doubt about her. My instinct told me just one thing about her: that she was good and that she loved me. If I was wrong about that, then I was wrong about everything. And maybe I was.

I didn't know anything. All I had was guesses. Guesses which, when you probed them and tried to follow them out, became ridiculous.

If Eggleston was wrong about the pardon, then most of my conjecturing collapsed. Doc might be my friend. It could be that he had become aware that we were being pressed toward a dangerous situation and that he intended to avoid it at all costs.

Oh, hell, though. That couldn't be right. It—

I gave up. I undressed and got in bed. Yes, and I went to sleep. You can only think so much and I was far ahead of my quota for the day.

The next day was the beginning of my second thirty-day period on parole. I called Myrtle Briscoe's office from a drug store, and asked what time I should report. She told me curtly that I needn't bother to come in—unless there was something I wanted to tell her.

I said there wasn't. She banged down the receiver.

It wasn't much after nine when I reached Madeline's apartment, and she was still in bed. Instead of coming to the living room door, she stuck her head out the other one, the one to her bedroom.

She closed it after me, gave me a fiercely affectionate hug and flung herself down on the bed again. She was wearing white sleeping shorts and a white sleeveless pullover.

She sprawled out on the pillows, raised her legs straight in the air, and grinned at me impishly.

"Guess I'll just stay here all day," she announced.

"All alone?" I said.

"Guess I won't either." She let her legs down, sat up and yawned. "So-oo tired. Make me some coffee, huh, honey?"

"All right," I said.

"I'll get into something while you're gone. So you won't be thinking evil thoughts."

I told her I never had such things, and went on back to the kitchen.

I put a pot of coffee on the stove, and slipped a couple

of pieces of bread into the toaster. While they were getting ready, I put a napkin on a tray, laid out marmalade and butter, and sliced an orange. The whole business didn't take more than five minutes. I was pretty practiced in getting her breakfast.

I picked up the tray and started for the bedroom. And, then, I halted there in the kitchen door and stood staring. The bedroom door was still open, as I had left it, and I could see her almost as plainly as though I'd been in the room with her. And what I saw sent a cold chill of shock along my spine.

The sleeping trunks and pullover lay on the floor at her feet. She'd got into a pair of thin white panties, and her hands were behind her, working at the clasp of her brassiere. She was completely lost in thought. She wasn't thinking about dressing, but about something—someone—and those thoughts were anything but pleasant.

Always before, even when she was serious, she'd appeared gay, good humored, light hearted. I'd never seen her any other way. *She'd never let me see her any other way.* And now not a vestige of that gaiety and good humor remained. I could hardly believe it was the same girl, the same woman—this woman whose face was a hideous and sinister mask of hatred.

I stepped back into the kitchen, and waited a minute or two. Then I began to whistle and started for the bedroom again.

"Well," she said, as I put the tray down on a reading stand. "What took you so long?"

"Oh, I took my time," I said, carelessly. "I didn't want to catch you undressed."

"No-o!" she said. "I'm sure you wouldn't want to do that."

I poured coffee and sat down on the bed with her.

She'd put on a pair of slacks and a sweater and was propped up on the pillows, her knees drawn up.

"Good," she said, nibbling on an orange slice. "Very good."

For the first time since I had met her, I found it difficult to talk. To respond to her aimless, impish chatter. It was grotesque in the light of what I had just seen. I had the impression of being drawn into a game while a flood tide rose around my neck.

She finished eating, and I lighted a cigarette for her. My hand trembled a little as I held out the match, and she steadied it with her own hand.

"What's the matter with you this morning, Pat?"

"Matter?"

She didn't say anything. She merely lay back, waiting, her brown eyes inscrutable.

"I've been a little worried," I said. "Maybe that's it."

"Worried about what?"

"About what's going to happen to me. About what is happening to me."

"Is?"

"Yes," I said, and I told her about the car and my talk with Myrtle Briscoe. At some point in the telling, she suddenly sat up and gripped my fingers.

"Pat," she said. "Had you thought about telling Myrtle?"

"Yes," I said, looking squarely at her. "I've thought about telling her everything. About everyone and everything. It might send me back to Sandstone, but I think I'd have plenty of company on the trip."

"You might"—she released my fingers— "Why don't you do it?"

Her voice was flat, her gaze as steady as mine. I'd made a threat and what it had got me I didn't know. Advice—or another threat.

"I'm sorry," I said. "You're the only person I know to turn to, and turning to you doesn't seem to do any good. There's no reason why it should, of course, why you should help me—"

"Do you really believe that, Pat?"

"I don't know," I said, "what to believe."

"No," she nodded, "and there's your answer to everything. You don't see anyone's problems but your own. You don't trust anyone but yourself. The fact that I won't tell you everything I know is interpreted to mean that I'm against you. That's all you can see."

"I don't think that," I said.

"Yes, you do, Pat. And you're wrong in doing it. I haven't told you any more than I have because it isn't a good thing for you to know it. You'd blunder into something that you're not big enough to handle."

"I'm supposed to sit still and do nothing?"

"That's about it." Her face softened. "That has to be it for the present, honey. Whenever there's anything to be done, I'll let you know."

She squeezed my hand, and then she sat up and put her arms around me. She drew me down to the pillows, her cheek against mine, her lips moving against my ear.

"Poor red-haired Pat," she whispered. "He mustn't worry any more. In just a little while now ... all his troubles will be over."

18

The trap was snapping shut, I could feel it; a sensation of things rushing in on me from every side.

On Monday morning I stopped by the capitol to leave a bunch of the survey forms for Rita Kennedy. They were meaningless, of course, but appearances had to be kept up. Firmly entrenched as the highway department crowd was, even they were not taking unnecessary chances in an election year.

Rita Kennedy wasn't in, and she'd left word that she wanted to see me. I passed the day reading and driving, and went back to the capitol again that evening.

Rita took the forms I handed her with a crisp smile. "I hope I didn't inconvenience you by not being here this morning, Pat?"

"Not at all," I said.

"I'm glad to hear it. Is it raining out?"

I said it was. "At least, it's starting to."

"Oh, damn," she said. "I'll never be able to get a taxi this time in the evening. And, of course, this is one day when I wouldn't bring an umbrella."

"I've got my car here," I said. "The state car, that is. If you'd care to have me ..."

"I would," she said instantly. "Get down my coat

while I'm locking my desk. I want to get out of here."

I helped her on with her coat, and she gave my arm a little squeeze as we went out the door. She held onto my arm all the way down the corridor and out to the car. And she didn't exactly lean away from me.

"I've been meaning to have a talk with you for some time, Pat," she said, as I pulled the car away from the curb. "Can you talk while you're driving?"

"Why, yes," I said.

"Perhaps I'd better not have you. This traffic makes me nervous, and the rain makes it worse. We'll wait until we get to my apartment."

"Fine," I said.

"You don't have to hurry home for any reason?"

"Not at all."

"We'll wait, then. I won't keep you long."

"It'll be all right if you do," I said.

"I won't. Don't talk any more, please."

She gave me her address, and I kept quiet all the way. I stopped in front of a large apartment house, and a doorman with an umbrella ushered us to the door. An elevator shot us up to some floor near the top.

I don't know how many rooms there were in the apartment. But I know it must have been large and expensive. It was the kind of place you have when you like good things and have had the money to buy them for a long time.

A Negro maid in a white cap took our wraps, and Rita asked me what I'd like to drink.

"Scotch will do me fine."

"I'll have the same ... Sit down there by the fire, Pat."

I took a chair in front of the fireplace, and Rita came over and stood by the mantel, pausing on the way to arrange a vase on the grand piano. When the drinks came she nodded to me over her glass, lifted it, and set it down almost empty.

"Something tells me that's quite a bit better than they serve in Sandstone."

"Yes," I said, "it is."

"Don't be so sensitive about it," she said. "We went into your background thoroughly, Pat. Believe it or not, we're extremely careful about whom we hire in the highway department."

"You must be," I said; and she chuckled.

"I think you'll get along all right, Pat. If you'll come to your senses. Have you found yourself a new sponsor, yet? Burkman's out, you know."

"No," I said. "I didn't know he was out."

"Oh, yes. Losing the election is only a formality. We weren't positive when we took you on, and we never put the lid on until we are positive. Fortunately for you, and a lot of others."

I said, "Well—"

"We're the largest of all the departments; we have the most jobs. That enables us—the top handful—to perpetuate ourselves. If we see a likely looking candidate we may start handing him patronage, even though the election is a year off. When we see a man on the downgrade we shake him. We kick his jobholders out. We lick him with his own people, and let the new man in. We've shaken Burkman."

"And you're ... kicking his people out?"

"We've kicked them out. All except you. I thought we might make a trade with you."

"What kind of a trade?" I said.

"A job for some information."

"I don't have any information you could use."

"I'm probably a better judge of that than you are. We're curious. We think there may be straws in the wind that we can't see. Doc's taken a lot of trouble with you. He's pretty good at playing both ends against the middle, himself. What's the answer?"

I shook my head; I hardly knew her. This was going too far too fast.

"I don't know the answer," I said. "And I couldn't tell you if I did. Doc took me out of Sandstone."

"And he could send you back?"

"Yes. But I don't need threats to keep me from double-crossing my friends."

She nodded, smiling a little, as if she'd expected me to say that.

"I think a stretch in the penitentiary might do a lot of my acquaintances some good, Pat. Well, you can have the job, anyway. Another drink?"

"No, thanks," I said. "And perhaps you'd better not let me keep the job."

"Nonsense," she said. "You're being melodramatic; if you can pick up any valuable information around there, I'll split the proceeds with you. No. The only way you'll be able to help Doc is to give him part of your salary."

"I'll be glad to do that," I said.

"You're planning to stay with us, then. I wondered. You see, we watch car transfers very closely. I thought you might be going away."

"No, ma'am," I said. "It's an old car. I just bought it to knock around in."

"Oh? I understood that you were keeping the state car after hours."

"I am," I said. "What I'll probably do is fix up the one I bought in my spare time, and resell it."

"I see."

"I couldn't leave, Miss Kennedy. I'd be breaking my parole."

"So I understood," she said. "I wondered if you did. You'd have a great deal to lose by leaving, Pat. What would you gain?"

"Nothing. I'm not leaving."

She smiled, shaking her gray head slightly.

"Have you read a book called *Sappho*, Pat?"

"No—yes. Alphonse Daudet, wasn't it?"

"The hero had strong obligations too, if you remember. A career, a proud family. And all he had to gain was a harlot. An unusually lovely harlot—but aren't they all when a man falls in love with them?"

"I don't know what you're talking about," I said.

"I'm talking about Mrs. Luther."

I said, "Oh," and I think I sighed inwardly with relief.

"It would be very easy for you to be in love with her. I wouldn't blame you at all."

"But I'm not." She couldn't have heard anything. If there was that much talk, if it had already got to her...

"What would you do if I called you a liar?"

"Well," I smiled. "From you, I'd take it."

"Consider it said, then. You're the worst possible kind of liar."

"All right," I said.

"If I were you I'd do a great deal of thinking. Doc has never made any impression upon me except in a slippery sort of way, but he's gone through a lot for that wife of his and he won't give her up easily. There's a blind spot in every man; there's something he'd kill for. Leave Mrs. Luther alone. Don't have anything to do with her, and don't let her have anything to do with you."

"Maybe—" I hesitated, "maybe I don't see what you're driving at, Miss Kennedy. Mrs. Luther is inclined a little to make up to a man, whether the man is interested or not—"

"That isn't what I mean."

"Well—"

"Will you have another drink? I'm going to have to start dressing in about five minutes."

"No, thank you." I got up. "I appreciate your talking to me, Miss Kennedy," I said. "But you seem to have heard something that just isn't true. Someone's been misrepresenting me to you," I said.

"No one misrepresents anything to me."

"Well, I don't blame you for not wanting to stick your neck out. But if there's talk going around—"

"Goodnight, Pat. This conversation was strictly between us. You don't need to worry about that."

"What do I need to worry about?"

"Goodnight."

She smiled, but she sounded angry; or, rather, disgusted. It was almost as if she said, "Good God!"

I rode back downstairs and jumped in the car, slamming the door after me. It was late, now, and the rain made the night darker. I didn't know he was there until he spoke—until a match flared and raised up to a face beneath a slouch-brimmed hat.

I recognized him just in time to keep from swinging. Or rather to stop the swing I'd started.

"That," I said, settling back on the seat, "is a good way of getting killed, Mr. Eggleston."

"There is no good way of getting killed, Mr. Cosgrove. I see your point, though. I didn't realize I was quite so invisible."

"How did you find me?"

"Find you? You mean you're trying to avoid discovery?"

"You know what I mean."

"Yes. Well, it wasn't a task that strained my professional capabilities. Whoever got your parole would have strong political connections. Those connections would almost certainly be used in getting you a job. A few hours of observation, a few discreet inquiries—and here I am."

"You followed me from the capitol."

"So. I thought it would be better, say, than calling you at Dr. Luther's."

I turned the switch key, and stepped on the starter. His cigarette arced down to the floor, and I heard his heel grind it out. I heard something else, too.

"Going some place, Mr. Cosgrove?"

"I thought I'd drive some place where we could talk," I said.

"We can talk very well here. But drive on, if you like. I only hope you will do nothing that will make it necessary for me to shoot you."

"Hell," I laughed, and I shut off the motor. "Why would I do anything like that?"

"Because you might feel I was dangerous to you, whereas I'm actually your buckler and your shield. I have much more to sell you than silence. Something even more golden, from any standpoint."

"Let's hear it," I said.

"A question or two, first. And please, for your own sake, be very accurate with your answers. Number one: What prompted Dr. Luther to get your parole? Did you talk with him while he was visiting Sandstone, or—"

"I wrote him a letter. Him and probably a hundred others. He was the only one to respond."

"Oh, good. Very good. You had no acquaintance with him whatsoever, right?"

"Right," I said. "I've already told you that."

"Question number two: How long was it after you wrote this letter before Dr. Luther acted in your behalf?"

"I don't know exactly. As I say, it was one of a number of letters, and I didn't keep track of them. I think it must have been around three months."

"I think it must have been, too, Mr. Cosgrove. In fact, I'd take an oath on it. Now—"

"Just a minute," I said. "How do you know that?"

"Because the time corresponds with another act—a series of acts, I should say—by Dr. Luther. Acts which provide the motive for your parole. Now, question number three: Has anything happened which would incline you to believe that you might be forced into a disastrous quarrel with Dr. Luther?"

"Yes," I said.

"Mrs. Luther?"

"Mrs. Luther."

"I don't believe I've had the pleasure of meeting the lady. Is she a raving beauty—the kind to successfully inspire a mortal quarrel?"

"Not for my money," I said. "But a lot of men would be crazy about her. You've probably seen her type. Tall, blonde, beautiful. And a bum."

He grunted. With surprise, it seemed. But when he spoke it was in his usual flat monotone.

"Well, that's about all, Mr. Cosgrove. Except for a rhetorical question. Have you dwelt any on the fact that Dr. Luther is now approaching the end of his political career, and that he must have seen the beginning of that end at about the time he received your letter?"

"I've thought about it a great deal," I said.

"And?"

"All right," I said, "I'm curious. I'm more than curious. What have you got to tell me?"

"Nothing more, Mr. Cosgrove. Until I'm convinced, in a very concrete manner, that my words will be appreciated."

"How much?"

"Five hundred."

"I haven't got it."

"A technicality. You can get it. Any man who's done as much time as you have in a place like Sandstone knows how to get money."

"You think I'm going to—"

"I think you're going to do whatever is necessary to get that five hundred."

"What are you going to tell me for the five hundred?"

"The answer to your riddle. How to keep Patrick Cosgrove alive and at liberty. When you know what I know—and make certain parties acquainted with that fact—your troubles will vanish even as the legendary snowball in hell."

"I'm pretty much mixed up," I said. "I don't see how. . . . How soon do you want the money?"

"Not later than tomorrow night. Say six o'clock."

"That isn't much time."

"I don't think you have very much, Mr. Cosgrove. From the way things are shaping up, I think your time is running out very fast. Unless you know what I know by tomorrow night, I don't think it will be of much value to you—or to me."

"But six o'clock," I said. "Something might come up that I couldn't get away that early. Could you make it after dinner, around eight?"

"That will be after dark," he said. "The other tenants will be out of their offices."

"What of it?"

"That's right. What? I'll be expecting trouble from you. Expecting it, Mr. Cosgrove. So I wouldn't bring anything with me, if I were in your place, but the money."

"Oh, hell," I laughed. "What would it get me?"

"Eight o'clock, then."

"I'll be there."

I'll be there before eight. I'll be there when you get back from your dinner.

20

Doc was backing his car out as I stepped off the porch, and I stood and waited for him to pass. He stopped and called to me, smiling.

"How's the job going, Pat?" he said. "Haven't kicked you out yet, have they?"

"Why, no," I said, showing a proper amount of surprise at the question. "Were they supposed to?"

"Maybe not. It may be a little early yet. They haven't said anything to you about Burkman, eh?"

"Not a word." I shook my head. "Is there some trouble?"

"We-ell—" he hesitated, "nothing that you need to worry about. We'll have to get you a new sponsor, but that shouldn't be difficult. Any number of the boys should be glad to come through for you."

"Fine," I said. "I'm glad to hear it."

"But I suspect we should be getting you a little better acquainted. Suppose you make it a point to be on hand tomorrow night. Around eight o'clock. I'm having a group in at that time."

I said I'd be there.

With a sigh of relief, I watched him back out the driveway and drive off. If he'd said tonight at eight I couldn't have met Eggleston. And if I missed out on that—

It would have been far better for me if I had missed out.

I drove out to the capitol building, circled around it, and headed back toward town. I backtracked on my trail several times, making sure that no one was following me, and reached the business district in about an hour. There I put the car on a parking lot and went to a picture show.

I left the show by a side street exit, ate lunch, and spent a couple of hours at the public library. After that I did some shopping.

I bought a small but strong pair of wire snips, a roll of adhesive tape, a pair of gloves, and a pocket flashlight. All in different stores. I went into a public toilet, unwrapped the articles and stowed them away in my pockets. I came out to the street again and sauntered slowly toward the market district.

It was now a little after five in the afternoon.

Catty-cornered to the building in which Eggleston had his offices was a workingman's bar. It was a grimy unattractive place, unpleasantly but effectively advertised by its odor of stale beer and fried fish. I wouldn't have eaten in it for pay, and I was sure Eggleston wouldn't.

I sat down at the bar, near the entrance, and ordered a drink. I glanced out the fly-specked window.

The view wasn't as good as I'd liked to have had. I could see the windows of Eggleston's offices, but I couldn't see the entrance to the building. That was on the side street, back near the alley.

I sipped my drink, waiting, watching his office windows. I didn't think he'd seen through my plan. It seemed to me that if he had he'd have said so, since it would get him nothing to let me go ahead. He might not go out to dinner, of course. In that case, I'd have to think of something else.

At six o'clock lights started coming on in the building. Some of them stayed on, but most went off after a few minutes. The shades at Eggleston's windows were drawn, and I had to stare hard to determine whether the lights were on or not.

At last, around six-thirty, when it was getting dark, I saw the broken lines of light around the shades. I saw them just in time to see them disappear. That left all the offices on his floor dark. It was better than I had hoped for.

I waited fifteen minutes more, then left the bar.

There were two elevators in the building, but only one was running at this time of night. I began looking at the office directory.

"Help you with somethin', mister?"

I shook my head without looking around.

He muttered something under his breath, and his stool creaked as he sat down again. Then the elevator signal buzzed, and he said "Goddam" and he got up and rattled the control.

"Going *up*, mister!"

I didn't say anything and I didn't look around. He banged the door shut and the car went up. I jerked open the door to the stairs and raced up them.

At the third floor landing I heard the elevator coming down, and I waited until its lights flashed on the foyer and disappeared. Then I ran down the corridor and around the corner, jerking the gloves over my hands.

Eggleston's outer office, the reception room, had a long pebble-glassed transom extending from the wall to the door casing. A short metal chain at each end allowed it to hang open a few inches.

I cut the chains with the wire snips and let the transom drop gently inward. I swung myself up and through the opening. I landed inside, swinging my feet just in time to avoid crashing down on a chair. I pushed the chair beneath the transom, climbed up on it, and took out the adhesive tape. I moved the transom back in its original position and taped the chains together again.

I sat down and rested.

My wrist watch said seven o'clock now. Eggleston had been gone approximately thirty minutes. Since our appointment was for eight, he'd hardly return before another half hour. That left me a lot of time ... to do what?

I started to light a cigarette, then put the package and the match back in my pocket. He might notice the smoke. Someone might notice the flare of the match.

I turned the pencil-beam of the flashlight on my watch again. Thirty minutes or more and not much to do but wait. I didn't know what to look for. At any rate, he'd hardly leave anything like this on paper. It would be in his head, something he could tell me.

I wondered how hard it would be to make him talk.

I hefted the wire snips, and stood up. How close to the door could I stand without being seen against the glass? And which side would be best to stand on? Here on the left or on the other side, where I could be behind it when it opened?

Probably here. He might sense something and he'd be armed. I might not be able to get out from behind the door fast enough.

I sat down and waited. And gradually, I felt my head turning toward the right, toward the door of the inner office. It was closed and the office was dark, and of course he wasn't there. He wouldn't be sitting in there in the dark. He hadn't expected me to do what I had, so why would he be there?

I thought that one over, and my head kept turning toward the door. And finally I got up and walked over to it, and turned the knob.

It was unlocked.

I pushed it open slowly.

I ducked back and flattened myself against the partition, and then I moved away from it and stepped inside and flicked on the flashlight.

The beam moved across the desk. He was bent forward a little on his elbows; his hands lay on top of each other carelessly; and the chair was drawn close to the desk, holding his body against it.

He wouldn't be talking that night or any other. He was through talking for all time.

21

I knew what had happened before I looked at his head.
He had pulled the chair up close to the desk and put
his elbows on it, because he had wanted to count
something, money, and that was the natural way to
do it. He had sat there counting, his suspicions lulled
by the fact that the money had been paid quietly,
without argument. And then the person—the man or
woman—who had handed it over so readily . . .

I moved the flashlight. I couldn't see his face; his
chin was resting on his chest, and his hat was pulled
too low. But I could see his head, even with the hat on.
Part of it was oozing right out through the crown of
the hat. He'd never known what hit him.

I wasn't sorry he was dead. I'd seen good men killed
for no reason, and he hadn't been good or even fair.
He'd meant to collect from both sides, from one for
keeping quiet and from the other—from me—for
talking. I might have foreseen that he would try that.
The murderer had.

I walked around the desk and opened a drawer.
There was nothing in it but a pipe, a can of tobacco
and a half-empty pint of cheap whiskey.

If there was anything significant in the thin file of
letters, the dog-eared ledger, or the several dozen

receipted and unreceipted bills, I didn't know what it was. Probably there wasn't anything. I felt his pockets as best I could without moving him. I found a few pads of matches, a wallet containing his credentials, and six dollars, a package and a half of cigarettes and a fully-loaded .32 automatic.

I put those things back where I'd found them, and looked down at the desk. There was nothing on it but a day-to-day calendar. The date showing was the following day.

I didn't think anything of it for a moment. I turned away and looked around the room carefully, trying to find—I don't know what I was trying to find.

I looked down at the calendar again, and then it came to me. It wasn't a mistake. This was one day that Eggleston wouldn't have slipped up on.

I flipped back one of the little white leaflets. There was the date, today, and scrawled across it were two notations:

>   Mrs. Luth.   5:45
>   P. Cos   8:00

I pulled it loose from the staples and tore it into shreds. I went through the expired calendar slips and tore off a dozen or more of them. I dropped them into the sink, burned them into ashes and flushed them down the drain. One missing slip might mean something. A number of missing ones wouldn't.

The phone rang, and I jumped. I moved back from it automatically, and then I lifted it up, let it bang against the desk and held the receiver against my ear.

I waited. And whoever was calling waited. At last there was a whisper, "Mr. Eggleston?"

I couldn't tell whether it was a man or a woman. You can't tell with whispers. "The same," I whispered back.

"I can't talk very loud, Mr. Eggleston."

"I'm in the same position."

That sounded like him, I hoped.

"I'm sorry I couldn't keep our appointment, Mr. Eggleston. Personally. Was it all right?"

"I'm afraid it isn't," I whispered. "I'm afraid I'll have to insist that you come down."

"That's impossible."

I didn't say anything.

"Why is it necessary for me to come down?"

"I think you know why."

"You got the money, didn't you? You were taken care of?"

It wasn't going to work. I wasn't going to get him or her to come down. That left only one thing to do. Startle that whisper into a recognizable voice.

"Yes," I said, in a deeper whisper. "I'm all taken care of. I'm sitting here with the top of my head bashed in. Dead."

That didn't work either. There was a short silence. Then the receiver at the other end of the wire went down with a bang.

I pushed Eggleston's body back from the desk and searched it thoroughly. I might as well, I knew now, because I couldn't leave it here. The time of death couldn't be fixed exactly; thirty minutes or an hour would be about as close as the police could come to it. And that, since the real murderer would have a foolproof alibi, left me the only suspect.

There was a chance that the elevator boy wouldn't remember my loitering around the lobby. There was chance that he couldn't describe me if he did remember. But I, a man on parole, a man with a criminal record, couldn't take those chances. Someway I'd have to get the body out of the building. Hide it. The river would probably be best.

My search produced nothing but a few keys, some coins and another partly filled package of cigarettes. I dropped them back into his coat pocket, and stood back studying him. He'd bled very little, and that had been absorbed by his hat and hair. He wasn't bleeding at all now. There were no stains to clean up. Nothing to do but get him out of there.

That was all.

I tested the outer door and found it unlocked; I could have walked in instead of climbing. I glanced at the snipped chains of the transom. They would be discovered and arouse comment, but without the body they didn't mean anything. In time, of course, Eggleston's absence would arouse inquiries. But by that time, I hoped, I would have the riddle of Dr. Luther solved. I would know what Eggleston had known and, hence, who had killed him.

But that was something to work out later, when, perhaps, I had more to work on. Right now Eggleston's body had to be got out of there.

I opened the door, glanced out, and let it close again. Going back into the other office, I picked the body up in my arms, carried it to the door and pulled it open with my fingers. It was still clear outside. The other offices were quiet and dark.

I let the door close behind me and walked swiftly down the corridor to the turn. I stuck my head around it; all clear there too. I broke into a trot; moving as rapidly as I could with the dead weight I was carrying.

I reached the elevators, and set the body down in front of the door of the unused one. Panting, I pressed the signal button. My car was parked two blocks away. I needed a total of at least five minutes. Two minutes to get there. A minute to get the car off the lot. Two minutes to get back.

Just five minutes.

I heard the elevator door clang at the bottom of the shaft. Cables whined. I flattened myself against the wall and waited.

Light bobbled on the corridor as the elevator moved past and then came back to the landing. The door rattled and banged open.

"Going down," came a sullen snarl.

I held my breath, clenched my fist into a hard, leather-covered ball.

"Going"—he stuck his head out—*"ugh!"*

My fist came up hammer-like beneath his chin. His head went back, and then he toppled straight forward. I caught him, stretched him out on the floor of the car and felt his heart. The beat was fast but steady. Aside from a cut lip, where his teeth had snapped into it, he wasn't hurt.

The door had closed automatically. I opened it again, holding it with my foot while I reached out and dragged Eggleston inside. A moment later, having worked out the simple controls of the elevator, I brought it to a stop between two floors.

I sank down on the stool, brushing the sweat from my eyes. Almost instantly, the memory of that automatic door brought me back to my feet.

I couldn't prop the door open while I went after my car. Not with a dead man in one corner and a senseless one in another. There might not be much traffic in the building at night, but obviously there was some. Otherwise an elevator wouldn't be in operation.

Feeling through the operator's pockets, I found what I was looking for, something I'd seen used at various times. It was a short thin piece of metal rod. An elevator "key." Thrust through two small overlapping holes in the elevator doors, it permitted them to be opened from the outside.

I dropped it into my pocket, shut off the lights and slowly lowered the car to the first floor. Looking through the small glass door panel, I saw that the lobby was empty. I stepped out and the door snapped shut, and I hurried away.

When I got back, I made a careful left turn and drew up just short of the building entrance. The street was unlighted. The only illumination came from the dimmed lights of the lobby.

I set the throttle so that the motor was barely turning over. Then, easing the left door off the catch, I slid out the right one, leaving it open behind me.

I stepped toward the entrance—and I stopped. My heart stopped for a moment. Someone was in there. Pounding on the elevator door. Pounding and, now, shouting.

I forced myself to walk on. I walked on, slowly, glancing inside as I passed. I couldn't get a good look at him, and he didn't look in my direction at all. He was too busy with his angry pounding and kicking on the elevator door.

I waited a moment at the alley, and turned and walked back again, Time! I'd run over my margin of safety minutes ago. Even without that pounding, the elevator operator was due to come to his senses any moment. And if it kept on, if I couldn't get in there—

The racket rose to a thunderous crescendo. Then it stopped, and footsteps crossed the lobby, and there was another sound: The slamming of the door to the stairs. He'd given up. He'd decided to walk.

I ran for the entrance, glancing up and down the street. All clear. Thank God this building was where it was, that this was a side street. Racing through the lobby, I yanked the elevator key from my pocket and jammed it through the overlapping holes in the door.

From inside the car came a steady rattling buzz. Signal buttons. Someone wanted to come down. Several people from the sound of things. Probably some of them had already started to walk down. Were already on the stairs. And I couldn't wait. There'd be more. What if I was penned up there with a dead man, and—

Something was holding the door of the car, pressing against it. It wouldn't open. It opened a few inches, but—but—

The clatter of the signals was growing louder. And above it, from somewhere upstairs, I heard the vicious slamming of a door. Then another. Then voices calling to each other, and the hollow echo of footsteps coming downward.

The door slid open another agonizing inch. I dropped the key, got both hands into the opening and threw everything I had into one gigantic tug.

It grated and groaned—and then it shot open. And the elevator operator sagged through it. He'd revived partly. He'd been leaning against the door, holding it with his weight.

He fell forward, knees limp, head down. I gave him a swinging right. He shot backward into the car, struck the back wall, and fell face-forward to the floor.

Too hard. I hadn't meant to hit him so hard. But no time to think of that, now. No time to look at him.

I lifted Eggleston's body. I clawed the door open with one hand, and staggered outside. Only seconds, now. Only a few seconds to get the body into the car and get away. The steps on the stairs were rushing downward. They'd passed the second floor. Any moment the lobby door would open, and—

I ran toward the entrance. Only a few feet to go. Out of the lobby and across the walk into the car. Only a few feet and—and I couldn't make them. I couldn't go back and I couldn't go forward. Someone had stepped into the entrance.

A blue-uniformed cop.

22

He had been looking at something down the street as he stepped into the entrance, and his head was still turned now. I stopped dead in my tracks, paralyzed for the moment with shock and fear. Then, as his head started to turn toward me, I acted. I did the only thing there was to do.

I ran forward and hurled the body at him.

It struck him high in the chest, obstructing his vision—I hoped—and bowling him over backwards. He yelled and grappled with it blindly, and I darted around to one side and sprang for the car.

I brought my foot down on the accelerator, grabbing at the doors. They banged shut and the motor stuttered and roared and the car leaped ahead.

As I shot past the entrance, I caught a confused picture of two figures rolling on the sidewalk and another running toward them from the lobby. Then, I was out of that block and in the middle of the next one, nearing the second intersection, and the speed indicator read seventy miles an hour.

Somehow I got control of myself. I brought my foot down on the brake, and the car skidded perilously. I eased up on it for a split second, then brought it down again. At something near the legal speed limit, I swept through the intersection.

Fortunately, there were no traffic lights this far down and very little traffic. At least it was fortunate at that particular moment. In the long run, I knew, safety would lie where the traffic was thickest. I rolled on, slower and slower, breathing heavily, nervous sweat rolling down into my eyes.

I turned left at the next corner, entering an arterial street which led through the center of the downtown district. Not until then did I hear, far to the rear of me, the shrill clatter of a police whistle.

Moving automatically with the traffic, I drove through town. I was safe, but for how long? And who could I turn to for help, if I needed it—if that cop had spotted my license plates or if the elevator operator could describe me?

Wrapped in thought, driving blindly, I came out on the other side of the business district. I passed an apartment house, and suddenly I thought of Hardesty. He lived in this neighborhood, and he wanted something from me. The man who wants something is a good man to drive a trade with.

I found his address, an apartment hotel near the park, and parked my car across the street from it. The lobby clerk was working the switchboard, his back to me. I got into the automatic elevator, punched a button and rode up.

Hardesty came to the door in a dressing gown. He started to smile when he saw me. Then his eyes widened, and the smile faded into a startled frown. And he grabbed my shoulder abruptly and jerked me inside.

"Why the hell did you come here?" he snarled, slamming the door. "Haven't you got sense enough to—" Breaking off with an angry curse, he strode across the room to a large radio and flicked the switch.

It burst into raucous sound, and cursing again, he turned down the volume. "Listen," he said, curtly.

I listened.

"... additional information on the man who, a few minutes ago, beat an elevator operator in the Haddon Building unconscious, murdered a tenant of the building and escaped after slugging a police officer with the dead man's body.

"The murderer is about six feet four inches tall and has red hair. His complexion is swarthy; he is well-dressed; he is believed to be driving a late-model coupe with an out of state license. The elevator operator believes him to be the same man he saw loitering around the building earlier in the evening. No motive is yet apparent for ..."

The radio switch clicked.

Hardesty looked at me, grinning; smiling in affable apology.

"Sorry, Pat," he said. "I was listening to that when you knocked, and I thought—well, that red hair and all ..."

His voice trailed off, and he frowned again.

"Oh," he said, softly. "So it was you."

"I'm the man they're looking for," I nodded. "But I didn't kill anyone. I found the body. I was afraid the murder might be pinned on me so I tried to get it out of the building."

I gave him a brief account of what happened. He listened absently, with only a pretense of interest, but his face cleared.

"Well," he shrugged, "they seemed to have you tabbed wrong, anyway, even to the license on your car. The only thing they've got right is your hair and they can't haul in every red-haired man in town."

"They can haul in all those who have criminal

records," I said. "And that elevator operator could identify me if he saw me again."

"I doubt it." He shook his head. "And how are the police going to know that the murderer had a criminal record? No, just sit tight for a few days, keep out of that neighborhood, and you'll be all right. Three or four days from now that elevator jockey wouldn't know you, even if you did have the bad luck to run into him."

"I hope you're right," I said.

"I'm sure of it, Pat. I know how those things go. It would have been better of course if you'd just walked out after you discovered the body. But that can't be helped now. Sit down and have a drink. I think you could use one.

"Now," he said, when he had poured two stiff drinks, "I wonder if there isn't something else you should tell me, Pat."

"For instance?" I tossed down my drink and poured another one.

"For instance, how you happened to be in this detective's office."

"I had an appointment with him," I said.

"I supposed you had."

"He was going to tell me what this was all about, why I was paroled from Sandstone."

"I see." He sat with his arms on his knees, bent forward a little, the glass cupped in his hands. There was a faint smile on his lips. "He was going to tell you something. He got killed. What conclusion would you draw from that?"

"You mean I shouldn't be curious?"

"That's exactly what I mean, Pat. I—"

"I think you're wrong," I said. "I think I should be a damned sight more curious than I have been. The murder is proof that I'm playing blind in a game where a life means nothing. Before tonight I was just worried. Now I know that I've *got* to find out what's going on."

"Oh?" he said, softly. "How do you propose to go about that, Pat?"

"I've already got an opening wedge. Mrs. Luther had an appointment ahead of me tonight. I think it's safe to assume that what Eggleston knew was about her."

"Mmm," he took a sip of the whiskey. "Go on."

"But she didn't keep that appointment. She told someone else about it and whoever that was came and killed Eggleston. In other words, her escort wasn't just important to her. In fact"—I hesitated, "it wasn't as important to her as it was to others, the murderer, for example."

"How," he said, "do you figure that?"

"Because she didn't handle it herself. It wouldn't have meant enough to her to commit murder, and murder had to be done. Therefore she wasn't allowed to keep the appointment."

"I see. Good reasoning," he nodded.

"Not very," I said. "Or you wouldn't say so. It all rests on the assumption that it was Mrs. Luther who telephoned there to the office tonight. I'm sure now that it wasn't."

He laughed and made a pass at slapping me on the knee. I drew my leg back.

"This isn't getting you anywhere, Pat," he said, sobering. "I told you I'd straighten everything out for you when the proper time came. Now, why don't you just forget it all for the present and we'll have a good talk some day soon when you're not so upset?"

"I'd like to know now," I said. "What do you want

with me? You and Doc and whoever's working with you?"

"I'm sorry, Pat. I—"

"Dammit," I said. "You're going to have to tell me sometime. You want me on your side of the fence, and I can't be there unless I know your plans. Now what is it?"

"You're a very smart young man, Pat. Far too shrewd for my liking."

"Thanks," I said.

"And I won't be ready for you to act for several weeks yet. Probably a month or so. If I explained things now, well—you see why I can't. Why take chances, particularly when I don't have to?"

"I see," I said. "You want to spring it on me suddenly. Without giving me a chance to think. I'll have to jump one of two ways and yours will look the best."

"Well, Pat?"

"You want me to kill Doc," I said. "Why?"

"Now, Pat"—he laughed nervously—"where do you get that idea?"

"All right," I said. "I'll kill him. I've had about all I can take. I'm going to do it tonight and then I'm skipping out."

"Pat!" He gripped my arm. "You mustn't. Not now. I mean—I—"

I shook off his arm, grinning at him. "Not now," I said. "But later. That's it, isn't it? You do want me to kill him. Let's have the rest of it."

"I've got nothing more to say, Pat. You'd better leave."

I nodded and got up. And then my hand went out in a stiff-arm, and he shot backwards off of the ottoman. I dived over the coffee table and on top of him, straddling his chest.

I grabbed up a whiskey glass and struck the rim against the coffee table. Part of it fell away, and I gripped it by the base, holding the long jagged splinters above his face.

His eyes rolled, and he stopped squirming.

"All right," I said. "I'm waiting."

"This"—he gasped—"this won't get you anywhere, Pat."

"Talk."

"Don't talk," said a voice behind me, and something hard and round and cold pressed against the back of my neck. "Betcha I'll shoot if you don't get up from there, honey. Betcha."

23

I dropped the glass and stood up, my hands raised. I turned around. She was grinning that cute crinkled grin, and her brown eyes were dancing with gay good humor.

"Whatsa matter, baby? Aren't ums glad to see mama?"

"God!" I said "God Almighty!"

"Poor, poor baby. So sweet and trusting and obliging with Madeline ... and all for a little petting. He didn't even get to sleep with her."

"No," I said. "I didn't. I've got that to be thankful for at least."

"Tsk, tsk," she said, grinning again. "Sour grapes, don't you think so, Bill?"

"Very sour," said Hardesty.

He had risen from the floor and kicked the glass into the fireplace, and now he moved over to her side and put his arm around her.

She leaned against him, her crisp brown hair brushing against his neck. She took his hand into one of hers and raised it up and pressed it tightly against her breast.

"There," she said, comfortably. "Hold the gun, will you, Bill? It makes my li'l fingers tired."

Hardesty took the gun and dropped it into his pocket. "We won't need that," he said. "Pat's ready to listen to reason, aren't you, Pat?"

"Reason," I said. "Reason."

"I'm sorry, boy," he said, and he sounded like he meant it. "Some things you can only do the hard way and this is one of them. You've never had a chance. You've been licked from the start."

"So I see," I said, dully.

"Doc knows you've been seeing Madeline. You were supposed to see her. You were bound to see that something was wrong, to be disturbed about it. It was Madeline's job to keep you from taking any action. Let you take it out in talk, more or less."

"Never mind," I said. "I understand. I guess I've understood from the beginning. I just wouldn't let myself believe it was true."

Madeline's grin faded. "I didn't want to hurt you, Pat. I didn't want you to get hurt. I told you to see me before you did anything, and you promised you would. If you'd kept that promise, this wouldn't have happened."

"I don't think you'd better say any more," I said. "I'm afraid if you keep on talking to me I'll try to kill you, and nothing will stop me but being killed. You don't want that. Yet. It would spoil your plans."

Hardesty shook his head, sympathetically. "We are sorry, Pat, believe me. I hope there's no hard feelings?"

"Over her?" I laughed shortly. "All right, I'm going now."

"Like another drink first?"

"No," I said and I started for the door.

Madeline's voice stopped me.

"Wait, Pat! No, wait, this is business! ... Bill, maybe we should tell him, now. That car, I'm worried about that. Doc shouldn't have bought it so soon."

"You mean the one for—for Pat's birthday?" Hardesty made a gesture of disgust. "Of course, he shouldn't have, but you know Doc. He's always got to be a jump ahead of everyone else, even if he jumps in the ditch."

"But this is different. He wouldn't go in for gestures at a time like this. I've got a feeling that—"

"Nonsense. This Arnholt deal breaks tomorrow night. It'll take him at least a month to wind it up, follow it through the legislature and collect. How could he—he—"

Their eyes met, and he jerked his head at me. She nodded slowly.

"I suppose you're right. We'll be in a terrible spot if you aren't."

"Of course, I'm right," said Hardesty. "Pat, I don't want to seem discourteous, but perhaps..."

I heard a suppressed laugh as I went out the door.

...I drank a great deal of whiskey that night, and the more I drank the more sober I became.

Around midnight, when the stuff was virtually running out my ears, I went into the bathroom and vomited for what seemed like hours. When it was all out of me, I started drinking again and I kept on until I fell asleep.

In this fine house I went to bed drunk, with my clothes on, for the first time in my life.

24

A LONG hot and cold shower and a close shave did wonders toward pulling me together. Afterwards, I had one short drink and got the morning paper from beneath the door.

Eggleston's picture and a half-column story about him were on the front page. Since the dead man had not been robbed, it was believed that:

> ...the private detective, long a familiar figure in divorce court proceedings, may have unearthed secrets which someone— probably a client—felt it unsafe for him to know.
>
> "I'm almost certain that our tall red-haired stranger and the murderer are the same man," Det. Lt. Rube Hastings declared. "Probably he only intended to throw a scare into Eggleston. Judging by his actions, I'd say that was what he had in mind. He walked up to the office, fearing perhaps that the elevator operator might want to accompany an after-hours caller. But he didn't mind being seen by the operator, as he would have if he'd contemplated murder.

"Something made him decide that he'd have to kill Eggleston, or perhaps he lost his temper. Then he realized that he'd have to get the body out of the building. The time of death could be approximated, and his presence in the building could be established. The only solution was to remove the body and hide it.

"The facts that the murderer apparently was well acquainted with Eggleston and feared identification prove that he is a local man who intends to remain here," according to Hastings. He was unable to explain why a permanent resident of the city was driving a car with an out-of-state license, but...

He wouldn't be unable to explain very long. Not if he was only half as bright as this story made him out to be. This was Capital City. There were hundreds of cars here with official license plates, the white plates with the square S at each end. That cop last night had only got a glimpse of my plates, and he'd put them down as belonging to some other state. But he wouldn't be long in changing his mind, having it changed by Det. Lt. Hastings.

I got the wallet out of my trousers and counted the money it contained. Only nine dollars, but there was a hundred and fifty more in the drawer of my writing desk. Doc had said it would be right there until he could get time to go to the bank with me.

A hundred and fifty-nine dollars. I could travel quite a ways on that if I had to.

I took a look at the clock, scooped up the clothes I had worn the night before and put them in the closet. The elevator operator had said I was wearing a dark suit—it was blue—black shoes—they were tan—and a gray hat—correct. I laid out a brown hat, a light gray suit, and brown-and-white oxfords.

I finished dressing and picked up the paper again. Another front-page picture and story caught my eye:

PHALANX LEADER SPEAKS TONIGHT

Fanning Arnholt, president of the National Phalanx and authority on subversive activities, will open his state-wide lecture series tonight with an address at 8:30 in Orpheum Hall.

Speaking on "Our Schools—Battleground of the Underground," Arnholt is expected to launch an all-out attack on a large group of textbooks which he claims are subversive. His appearance here is sponsored by local chapters of the Phalanx.

"The scarlet poison of Un-Americanism is flowing unchecked through the educational arteries of this great state," the noted patriotic leader declared upon his arrival here last night. "The antidote is an aroused citizenry which will force its legislative representatives into the proper and drastic action..."

So that Doc's crowd could make one last raid on the treasury.

I tossed the paper aside, and got up to help Henry with the breakfast tray. I told him to take everything back but the toast, orange juice and coffee. He fidgeted around the table, uncomfortably, doing everything twice.

"Something on your mind, Henry?" I asked.

"Well—" he hesitated, "you know that money you had, Mr. Cosgrove? There in your desk?"

I nodded. "What about it?"

"Well...I don't know whether you noticed yet or not, but it's gone. Dr. Luther took it. I thought I'd better tell you in case it slips his mind, since Willie and I are in your room so much."

"I understand," I said. "Did the doctor say why he was taking it?"

"No, sir. He just came in while I was cleaning up yesterday and got it."

"Thanks," I said. "Thanks for telling me, Henry. I won't mention that you said anything."

He gave me a grateful smile and left. I sat down at the table and munched at a piece of toast.

Nine dollars. Nine instead of a hundred and fifty-nine.

Sipping my suddenly tasteless orange juice, I knew what his explanation would be. Without looking around, I knew something else: that he was there in the room with me.

I don't know whether Henry had left the door ajar, or whether he had opened it very quietly. But he was standing there, leaning against the wall, staring at me reflectively through the thick-rimmed glasses.

I poured coffee, took a swallow of it, and half-turned my head. "Good morning, Doc. Coffee?"

"Good morning, Pat," he said, tiredly. "No, thanks."

He crossed to the bed and sat down. I turned my back again and went on with my breakfast, listening to the rattle of the newspaper.

"Pat."

"Yes, Doc?"

"I took the money you had in your desk. I thought we'd get that bank account opened for you."

"Fine," I said.

"I won't be able to get down today, though. Maybe we can make it tomorrow."

"Fine," I repeated. For I had expected that, and what else was there for me to say?

The paper rattled again, and there was another long silence. I drank my coffee and waited. Waited for him to read the story about Eggleston. To re-read it, perhaps, and then stare at me, looking at my hair and my clothes and remembering that I had been out late last night.

His voice was overly casual when he spoke.

"That's a nice-looking outfit you have on, Pat. I don't believe I've seen you in it before."

"Thank you," I said. "I thought I'd put on something light with the weather getting so warm."

I heard him light a cigarette. I even heard his slow meditative puffing.

"Why don't you drive your own car today, Pat? The battery's apt to run down if you don't drive it once in a while."

"I think I will," I said.

"You can put the state car here in the garage."

"Thank you. I'll do that."

He didn't speak again until I was drinking the last of my coffee, coffee that I didn't want. "By the way, Pat—that group I'm having in tonight. I'd like to use your room for them, if you don't mind."

"Anything you say, Doc," I said.

"We'll have to shift the furniture around a bit. Bring in some other chairs, and so on. If you can get your dinner outside it'll give us a chance to get everything ready before our guests get here."

"I'll be glad to help," I said.

"No, no. Henry and Willie can take care of everything. Just drop in at eight-thirty, or a few minutes before, rather. We'll be listening to a radio program, and I don't want anyone coming in after it's started."

I nodded and turned around.

He got up from the bed and sauntered toward the door, his eyes shifting so that they avoided mine.

"It's a tough world isn't it, Pat?" he said, in a tired flat voice.

"I used to think so," I said, "until you came along."

"What do you mean by that?" He flicked me a sharp glance.

"I was referring to all you'd done for me," I said. "The clothes, the job, the car, the home, the—well, the friendship you've given me. Unselfishly. Simply because I needed help. How can I feel it's a bad world as long as there's a man like you in it?"

A slow flush spread over his face. His lower lip drew back from beneath the protruding teeth.

"See you tonight, Pat," he said abruptly, and the door slammed behind him.

25

I CALLED Rita Kennedy's office.

I heard the sharp intake of her breath as I identified myself.

"I've got some more of the forms ready," I said. "I wonder if you'd like me to bring them in today?"

"I—don't bother," she said. "Just forget about them. And leave your car at home. We'll send someone to pick it up in a day or two."

"Oh," I said. "You mean I'm fired?"

"I'm sorry, Pat. Your check will be drawn up as of the close of business last night. We're unable to keep a man like you on the payroll. That...that isn't any reflection on your work, you understand."

I understood. There'd been inquiries already and Rita had answered them truthfully. *"A tall red-haired man? No, we have no one like that."*

"When will I receive the check?" I asked.

"It'll be several days, I'm afraid. I wouldn't wait on it."

"I'm broke, Miss Kennedy," I said.

"Broke!" she said. "Oh, good lord!" And then the concern went out of her voice and it was as clipped and curt as it had been at our first meeting. "That's too bad, Pat. I've done all I can. Much more than I should have."

"I know," I said. "I appreciate it."

"Don't bother to thank me for it. Ever. I haven't really done anything. I can't be expected to remember everyone who ever worked for us."

"Of course not," I said. "Good-bye, Miss Kennedy."

"Pat."

"Yes, ma'am?"

"Why did you do it?"

"I didn't. But I'll never be able to convince anyone of the fact."

"Did it have something to do with Doc?"

"Something," I said. "But I don't know what."

There was a short disbelieving laugh, and then the click of the receiver. That ended me with Rita Kennedy. As far as she was concerned, I no longer existed.

It was too late, now, to turn to Myrtle Briscoe. I couldn't go to her now, with a rap for murder hanging over me.

I drove downtown, cruising slowly past the building where Eggleston had had his offices. There wasn't anything to see there, of course. It was just something to do, some way of killing part of the long day ahead of me. Perhaps the last day of freedom I'd have. If I'd had my way I'd have stayed at the house. But Doc had made it very clear that he didn't want me there before tonight, and going back would mean bringing on a showdown. I was going to have to face one very soon, but there was no sense in jumping toward it. If Doc was certain that I was going to be washed up, he'd be the first man to throw a bucket of water. He'd feel that he had to, regardless of what his plans had been for me.

I turned the corner and idled the car up the street. I didn't feel like seeing a show. I didn't want to go to the library. I didn't want a drink either, but I had to do something. I ran the car on a parking lot, waiting in it while the attendant parked another car.

He came hustling up to me, a big smile on his face. And then the smile froze, and I knew that that was the last place in town I should have come to.

"Yessir," he said, trying to keep his voice casual. "How long you going to be, sir?"

"Just long enough to get a tire fixed," I said. "You fix them, don't you?"

"Well—uh—" He hesitated, staring at me.

"Well, how about it?" I said irritably. "I haven't got all day."

"Uh—" Some of the suspicion went out of his face and a flush of anger replaced it. "I can get it fixed for you, mister. You leave your car here, and I can have someone come and fix it."

"Oh, hell," I said. "I've got no time for that routine. Where's a garage near here?"

"Y-you—you work for the state, mister?"

"Work for the state?" I snorted. "Would I be driving a wreck like this if I worked for the state? Now do you know where I can get a tire fixed or not?"

He shook his head. Not in answer to my question but to the one in his mind. I wasn't the same guy; he wasn't going to be a hero.

I said something under my breath about dumbbells, just loud enough for him to hear it.

A couple of cars drove in just then, and he didn't have a chance to say anything more and I didn't have to. He trotted off sullenly, and I drove away. Within the next ten minutes, I drove a good five miles away.

I picked a quiet residential street, brought the car down to a steady fifteen miles an hour, and turned the radio to catch the police calls. I drove and listened until noon, and nothing came over the air. They weren't looking for me. Yet.

Around noon I stopped at a drive-in and had a hamburger and a bottle of beer in the car. The check brought my nine dollars down to less than eight-fifty. It also started me to thinking again about that one hundred and fifty that Doc had appropriated.

The more I thought about it the more certain I became that he'd taken the money to keep me from running away. He'd never intended to open any bank account for me and he didn't now. And then something had happened, or was going to happen, that made it unsafe for me to have that money longer.

It couldn't have anything to do with Eggleston, since he couldn't have foreseen how I'd be involved in that. And the only thing impending was the Fanning Arnholt scheme. So, somehow, he must be intending to use me in that. I was going to be used, and not several weeks from now but tonight.

I grinned to myself, thinking of Madeline and Hardesty. This was going to spoil their plans. The thing was going to explode on them before they were ready for it, and they'd have to do their own dirty work, whatever it was, instead of dragging me in on it.

They weren't going to like that. Not a bit. Hardesty in particular, with the secure and respectable position he held in the city, was going to hate being caught with his neck out. There'd be a blow-up between him and Doc and Madeline. I might get enough to clear myself of Eggleston's murder.

I wondered how Doc was going to wind up the Arnholt scheme tonight, something that even I could see should take two or three weeks. And I remembered those rare out-of-character glimpses I'd had of him, as on my first night out of Sandstone, and I knew exactly how he was going to wind it up. I felt certain that this, if nothing else, would bring on a quarrel with Madeline and Hardesty.

Madeline...

I tried not to think about her. When I thought about her I hated myself because, well, I couldn't hate her. I couldn't, no matter what she'd done or might do, and I knew I never could.

Slowly, the afternoon passed. I drove around until three and had more beer at another drive-in. And then I did more driving, still sticking to the residential streets, and around five o'clock I stopped at a neighborhood bar and restaurant.

I sat down at the end of the bar and had a ham sandwich, potato salad and coffee. It was a small, sidestreet place and I was the only customer. My ankles ached from the day's almost steady driving. I decided to kill some of my remaining time there.

After I'd eaten I had a brandy and dropped a few nickels in the juke box. I rolled dice with the bartender for drinks and won once and lost twice. By seven o'clock I was pretty well relaxed; as relaxed as I could be under my circumstances.

And, then, the cop came in.

He was a big, lumbering fellow with a broad red face, and he had little round unblinking eyes. He came through the door slowly, twirling his club as though it were an extension of his fingers, and stopped at the front of the bar. He looked the place over, walls, ceiling, floor and fixtures; studying it as if he might be considering its purchase. Then, he lumbered down to us.

The bartender finished his roll and passed the cup to me. I picked it up, numb fingered, and the cop swung the club up, caught it, and pointed it over his shoulder.

"That your coupe out there?"

"Yes," I said, easing my feet off the stool rungs. "It's mine."

"Buy it new?"

"No."

"How long you had it?"

"Not very long," I said.

He stared at me blank-faced. The club came down and began to twirl again.

"What'd you pay for it?"

"A hundred and seventy-five."

"Who'd you buy it from?"

"Capital Car Sales."

He caught the club under his arm, took a pencil from the side of his cap and a notebook from his hip pocket. He wrote in the book, his lips moving with the movement of his hand. He closed it, returned it to his hip and replaced the pencil in its clip.

"Been lookin' for a good cheap coupe," he said. "Think I'll go down and see them people."

And then he turned and lumbered out, the club spinning and twirling at his finger tips.

I had two more drinks, stiff ones, and got out of there.

At eight-fifteen I turned up the long wooded drive which led to Dr. Luther's house.

Three blocks from the house, a convertible was parked against the curb. I was swinging out to pass it when a woman stepped into the beam of my headlights and held up her arm.

Lila.

"Oh, Pat," she said, as I stopped beside her. "I'm so glad you came along. I seem to be out of gas."

"That's too bad," I said. "If you'll steer your car, I'll push it home for you."

"Oh, that's a lot of bother," she said, and she opened the door of my car and climbed in. "Let's just leave it here. I'll send one of the boys back after it."

I closed the door for her, but I didn't drive on. She could have walked home in five minutes. Why wait for me? For obviously she had waited for me.

I turned and looked at her, and she smiled at me brightly in the darkness. "Well, Pat? Hadn't we better be going?"

"Doc told you to wait there for me, Lila," I said. "Why?"

"Now what are you talking about, Pat?" she laughed. "I told you I was out of gas."

"Do you know what you're doing, Lila? Or are you just running blind, doing as you're told?"

She shook her head, not answering.

"Lila," I said. "I think you're pretty straight. I think you'd like to be straight. But you're mixed up in something damned bad. If you keep on, the same thing that happened to Eggleston may happen to you."

"Eggleston?" Her voice was puzzled. "Who's he?"

"You know who he was. The private detective."

"I don't know anyone named Eggleston—any private detectives."

"Don't hand me that," I said. "You had an appointment with him last night...and he was murdered."

"Murdered?" she said blankly. "And I had an appointment with him? You're joking, Pat!"

I grabbed her by the arms and started to shake her; and then I let go and slid under the wheel again.

"Yes," I said, "I was joking. Now I'll drive you home."

"I really don't know anything about it. Honest, I don't."

"No," I nodded. "You don't. Eggleston's appointment was with Mrs. Luther. You're not Mrs. Luther."

SHE gasped and whirled on me.

"That's not true! Why—why—" she laughed, a little hysterically, "I never heard of such a thing!"

"All right, then," I said, "we'll say that you *are* Mrs. Luther. You're Doc's wife and marriage doesn't mean a thing to you. You're Doc's wife and you killed Eggleston last night or you had him killed."

That got her; hit her hard from two directions. It hurt her pride deeply, and it frightened her even more.

"Y-you—you guessed it," she said, at last. "I didn't tell you!"

"No," I said. "You didn't tell me. Doc did. He told me enough so that I should have seen it. How did it start, Lila? Were you a patient of his?"

"N-not"—she shivered—"not at first. I met him on the train, years ago—about ten years, I guess it was—when he was coming here for the first time. I—I'd been losing a lot of sleep, and I thought I might be going crazy. He talked with me, and afterwards I felt better. And when he opened his offices here, I started consulting him. I—he found out what was worrying me."

"What was it?" I kept my voice gentle, sympathetic. "Had you killed someone?"

"My husband. I—I didn't mean to—I don't think I meant to—but I guess that doesn't matter. I was tired, of waiting on him, I suppose, and I gave him too much of the medicine. They all said I'd killed him. They couldn't prove anything, but they kept saying it. I had to leave there."

"And Doc picked up where your neighbors left off," I said. "He convinced you that you had committed murder. I imagine he even got you to admit it, didn't he?"

She turned and looked at me, eyes widening. "You sound like—like you don't think I—"

"Of course, you didn't do it intentionally," I said. "Doc wanted to use you so he made you believe you'd killed your husband. Let's see if I know what happened, then, after he had you start posing as his wife. He—"

"No need to guess about it, Pat," she said, and she told me how it had been.

Doc had used her in a kind of high class badger game with the capital big shots. He didn't take money. Money might have led to a charge of blackmail and, at any rate, the easy money crowd seldom had heavy cash assets. So, when Doc caught his "wife" in a compromising situation with one of the big boys, he simply demanded to be cut in on the political gravy. That gave him his "in," enabled him to get out of the game fast. For, of course, it couldn't be worked indefinitely. As it was, talk began to circulate that Lila Luther was too promiscuous to actually be so, and that Doc seemed jealous only when he could profit by it. His victims couldn't charge him with blackmail, but they could run him out of town if they learned the truth. They could fix it so that, even in the shadiest political circles, no one could afford to become involved with him.

"I guess that's why he hates me so much," Lila concluded. "It's been years since I've been of any use to him but he's had to go on keeping me. He's had to treat me as a man in his position would be expected to treat his wife. I guess, in the long run, I've gotten a lot more from him than I got for him."

"How have you felt about it, Lila?"

"I don't know, Pat." She shrugged wearily. "I don't know any more. I put up a fight at first, but then I just kind of gave up. I'm not very bright; there's no point in telling you that. There's no work I'm any good for, and Doc had that hold over me, and, well, I just gave up. I didn't know what else to do."

"Do you know what Doc's plans are about Fanning Arnholt?"

"Fanning Arnholt?" She looked blank.

"The textbook deal."

"I don't know anything about it, Pat. Really I don't."

I threw a few more questions at her, trying to trip her up. But she was telling the truth. She didn't know anything of Doc's plans. She simply did as she was told, and no questions asked.

"I'll tell you something," I said, "and I want you to believe me, Lila. You're on a hell of a spot. Almost as bad a spot as I'm on. Doc isn't going to be around any more after tonight. You're going to be left alone, without any money and probably even without a place to live, and you're going to be right in the middle of one of the biggest scandals that ever hit Capital City."

She turned on me, startled. Then, she laughed, incredulously. "But—how? Why? I mean—"

"I can't explain now. It would take too much time; it wouldn't make sense to you. But here's something to think about. Since you aren't Mrs. Luther, who is?"

"Who?" She laughed again. "Why—well, no one. I mean, Doc just made—"

"Huh-uh. He didn't make the story up. He'd know it would be checked. He was married under exactly the circumstances he said he was, and his wife followed him here after he reestablished himself. He's kept her out of the dirty work—as much of it as he could—and used you instead. And now that the elections are going sour...Well, what do you think is going to happen, Lila?"

"I..." She frowned, trying to think and getting absolutely nowhere. "I don't—Tell me what to do, Pat."

"You were supposed to pick me up here tonight?"

"Yes. I was supposed to make it look like—like we'd been out together."

It seemed like the showdown, but I couldn't be positive. And if I jumped the gun, there wouldn't be any proof. I could set the deal up only once, and if it fell through I'd never get another chance.

"Tell me what to do, Pat."

I hesitated. Then, I took a notebook and a pencil from my pocket. "Do exactly what you first intended to," I said. "But do this also. When—if—I give you the nod, excuse yourself and call this party. Tell her to go to—"

I hesitated again...To go to Doc's house? No. No, he couldn't leave from there. There'd be things he'd have to take with him—clothing, toilet articles and so on— and he couldn't take them from the house.

"...tell her to come to this address, and bring some help with her. Tell her to stake the place out and..."

I ran through it a couple of times, spelling it all out. Because it was simple enough, but so was she. I tore the page from my notebook, watched her tuck it into her purse and stepped on the starter.

I drove on to the house. I parked the car in the garage, and opened the door for her. She followed me up the drive, lagging a few steps behind; then, as we neared the porch, she caught up with me and linked her arm through mine.

She clung to it tightly, letting her long soft hip brush against me. We entered the hall, and she pulled me around suddenly and kissed me on the mouth.

I grinned and patted her on the arm. I didn't say anything. I didn't wipe off the lipstick.

It was just eight-thirty. Arm in arm, we went down the hall and into my room.

There were about a dozen people in the room. Doc was there, of course, and Hardesty. Then there was Burkman, Flanders and Kronup, and a couple of the textbook men. The others I didn't know, although I'd seen most of them around the house or the capitol from time to time.

My bed had been pushed against the wall, along with the desk, table and reading stand. Doc was sitting on a stool in front of the radio. The others were lounging in a half-circle of chairs facing the instrument.

The air was blue with cigar and cigarette smoke. Everyone except Doc had a glass in his hand.

Lila and I sat down in two straight chairs, the only unoccupied ones, and for a moment every eye was on us—and the room was completely silent.

Every eye was on us, and then on Doc, watching his startled scowl, the protruding teeth that bared suddenly, unconsciously it seemed, in anger.

He stared at us, turning the dial of the radio. "This is it," he said slowly.

And the announcer's quick, falsely excited voice filled the room:

"Ladies and gentlemen, we take you tonight to

Orpheum Hall where Mr. Fanning Arnholt, president of the National Phalanx, is speaking on 'Our Schools —Battleground of the Underground.' As you doubtless know, Mr. Arnholt has long been in the vanguard of those alert and courageous citizens who are fighting the good battle against subversive influences. He has—"

Then they were all staring at the radio which had suddenly gone dead.

"I don't know." Doc shook his head at their unspoken question. "The thing's working all right. It—"

"If you will stand by for just a moment"—it was the announcer again—"there seems to be ... Mr. Arnholt was right here on the platform with me a moment ago, but he seems to have been called away. I wonder—yes, there he is now! He's talking to some other gentlemen, and he looks quite—quite ill. And ... Stand by, please!"

The two textbook men looked at each other nervously. Someone said, "What the hell?" and there was a chorus of "Shhs." I glanced at Lila. I nodded. I hadn't known quite what to expect, but I knew this was the beginning of it. She got up and left the room quietly. And I saw, or thought I saw, a peculiar look in Doc's eyes. But he didn't say anything, and no one else seemed to notice her departure. They were all too interested in what was—or wasn't—coming from the radio.

It wasn't completely silent, now. We could hear the subdued roar of the audience, and the sound of several voices, apparently near the microphone. Two of them rose above the others:

"But Mr. Arnholt is the scheduled speaker ..."

"... isn't speaking ... we're paying for time ..."

"... all right. I'll take over."

The microphone popped and rattled, and the announcer came back again:

"Thank you for waiting, friends. Due to the unforeseen circumstances, which will be explained to you, Mr. Arnholt will be unable to address you tonight. I will now turn your over to Mr. Ralph Edgars, state president of the National Phalanx ... If you please, Mr. Edgars."

"Thank you," said another voice. "Uh—I didn't come here prepared to talk, folks, and I'm sorry that I have to. It's my job to tell you that I and the organization which I head in this state seem to have been pretty badly taken in ..."

He paused and cleared his throat, and the audience was as absolutely silent as this room where we sat. Even I, who had expected something like this, leaned forward, straining to hear:

"A few minutes before Mr. Arnholt was scheduled to speak tonight, a number of documents—or I should say photostats of documents—were delivered to me on this stage. I was amazed and dismayed to find that they cast serious doubts on Mr. Arnholt's motives for being here and on the entire series of talks he intended to make in this state.

"Briefly, these documents tend to prove that Mr. Arnholt was launching an attack on certain textbooks so that the books of rival firms might be adopted by the state in their place. In the absence of any satisfactory explanation from Mr. Arnholt, they did prove that.

"Under the circumstances, we local leaders of the Phalanx cancel his talk and offer you our apologies. For several reasons I will not now name the persons and firms who seem to be involved with Mr. Arnholt in this swindle. We have cleaned our own house, or will clean it shortly. It is not for us to take over the work of the courts. However, the names of these persons and firms will be made known to you shortly and proper action will be taken against them.

"The documents, the photostats, in my possession will be presented to the state attorney general tomorrow morning. And I am authorized to promise you that they will not be pigeon-holed or forgotten. I can promise you that ..."

Doc snapped the radio off.

He swiveled around on the stool, and waited.

Hardesty was the first to speak. For a moment he looked as sick and bewildered and frightened as any of the others. But, then, his face tightened and he forced a laugh.

"Well," he said. "There goes the ball game."

"There it goes," Burkman nodded slowly. "There g-goes—" And his pot belly trembled, and he put his hands over his eyes and began to cry.

Flanders laughed harshly. "What'd I tell you, Doc? Didn't I tell you that dumb son-of-a-bitch would screw himself up and us in the bargain? If you'd spent the same money and effort in the regular channels ..."

"How about the money, anyway?" It was one of the textbook salesmen. "Harry and me are both in for twenty-five hundred. How the hell are we going to explain a deal like this to our companies?"

"We ain't going to have to explain," said the other one, bitterly. "We're washed up. Out. We won't be able to sell a book in the southwest for the next twenty-five years."

Kronup shook his finger at Doc, snarling. "Money's the smallest part of it. We're not only out and facin' prosecution, but there's no one we can turn to. Now or any time. We ain't going to be able to keep a finger in;

we ain't going to be able to elect anyone that's halfway reasonable. What you've done, Doc, is put the whole damned reform crowd in office, put 'em there for good. And I'm sayin'—"

"Son-of-a-bitch," sobbed Burkman. "S-son-of-a-b-bitch. ..."

"Will you shut up?" yelled Flanders. "Doc, didn't I tell you that—"

"I'm talkin'!" Kronup shouted. "I say this phony psychologist made a deal! I say he sold us out!"

He shouted the accusation again, for they were all talking now; all shouting and snarling and growling at once. Frightened, surly, half-hysterical animals. Only Doc and Hardesty were silent. Hardesty was staring at Doc, a puzzled but bitter frown on his too-handsome face. Doc sat with his hands folded, looking down at the floor.

His mouth was working; he might have been muttering to himself. He might have been, but he wasn't. I was beginning at last to read his expressions. He was laughing.

His mouth stopped moving, and he looked up. He shook his head and the room grew quiet.

"Don't be a damned fool," he said coldly to Kronup. "How could I sell out? What would I get out of it? How could I make a deal with the reform crowd? There's no way they could give me anything, even if they wanted to."

"But—"

"But nothing," said Doc. "Anyway, we don't know how much of the deal was spilled to Edgars. A very little would be enough to get Arnholt and that's probably all Edgars has. He's trying to throw a bluff into us. If we sit tight and keep quiet, it may blow over."

There was a growl of dissent. "You don't believe that," said Flanders. "Arnholt's going to sing his head off. Regardless of what Edgars has or hasn't got in the way of documentary proof, it's going to be enough to wash us up."

"We're through and you know it," snuffled Burkman, angrily. "All we can do now is grab what we can before the ceiling falls in on us."

"Maybe you're right," Doc shrugged.

His quietness seemed to madden Burkman. He tried to speak and his throat choked with fury. And then he was pointing at me, shaking a trembling finger in my direction.

"You got some kind of scheme you're pullin' with that red-head, there. I don't know what it is but I know it must be good, the trouble you went to gettin' him out. You're cuttin' me in on it."

"You're cutting all of us in on it," corrected Flanders.

"I'm not," said Doc, levelly, "cutting anyone in on it. That deal is off. I'm letting Cosgrove return to Sandstone tomorrow."

27

I'd been expecting that, but the cold fact of its happening jolted me. I lighted a cigarette and my hand trembled.

"That's pretty sudden, Doc," I said. "Would you mind explaining?"

"If you need an explanation," said Doc, his voice clipped. "I've done a great deal for you. I intended to do a great deal more. And all I've asked of you is that you leave Lila alone. You wouldn't do it. You've carried on an affair right in front of me. Recently, you gave her the money to buy a car for you. You intended to jump your parole and leave town with her—leave me holding the bag both ways. I'm beating you to the punch."

A low murmur went around the room. Kronup cleared his throat with embarrassment.

"Say, that's too bad, Doc," he said. "I been hearing things out around the capitol, but—"

"Of course, you've heard things," I said. "Doc wanted you to hear them, and there was a certain basis of truth in them. Lila did buy that car for me. She has thrown herself at me. I've known the talk was spreading, but I didn't know what to do. I—"

"Well, I know what to do," said Doc, getting up

from the stool. "Gentlemen, I suggest that we get together in the morning and see what can be done about this Arnholt matter. Frankly, I can't think clearly enough tonight to discuss it."

They began to get up, brushing at their clothes and moving toward the door. A few stared at me; most of them deliberately avoided doing so. For the moment Doc's problem had become paramount to theirs.

"Just a minute," I said. "There's one thing you haven't told these gentlemen, Doc. Lila isn't your wife."

The movement toward the door stopped abruptly. They stared from me to Doc, and his jaw fell slack. And then Hardesty's voice boomed out, breaking the silence.

"So what?" he demanded reasonably. "He couldn't get a divorce from his wife, so he hasn't been able to marry Lila. That has no bearing on the matter. She's been more to him than most wives are to their husbands."

"Yes," said Doc. "A great deal more."

"Well, we'll all get along now," said Hardesty bluffly. "But I'd keep an eye on Cosgrove, if I were you. He isn't going to like going back to Sandstone."

"I'll keep an eye on him," said Doc.

They filed past him out the door. They were in a hurry to get out now. The news about Lila had value; some highly placed people would be very interested in hearing it.

They didn't know, as I did, that Doc wasn't going to be around to face the music.

At last, only Hardesty and Doc remained, and Doc took Hardesty by the arm and urged him toward the door. Hardesty hung back.

"I think I'd better have a little talk with Pat. Let him know how things stand."

"Later," said Doc, not looking at me. "Not now."

"I really think—"

"I don't give a damn what you think," said Doc. "I'll do the explaining when the time comes for it. Right now I want to get away from here."

Hardesty suddenly remembered something.

"You blew this Arnholt deal, didn't you? What the hell was the idea?"

"I'll explain about that, too," said Doc. "Now, come on. We're liable to have some callers as soon as that crowd starts telephoning. We can't afford to get tied up here."

"What about him?"

"He'll keep," said Doc, and he literally dragged Hardesty through the door and slammed it.

I fixed myself a drink and sat down on the bed. Faintly, I heard the last of the cars pulling away from the front of the house. Clearly, a few minutes later, I heard the smooth purr of Doc's sedan as it rolled out the driveway.

I finished my drink and lay back on the bed. I felt very comfortable, relaxed, for the first time since I'd left Sandstone. I'd told Lila to beat it as soon as she made the telephone call. There was nothing to do now but take things easy.

I lay thinking, grinning a little when I thought of the surprise that Doc and Hardesty were in for. And then I thought of Madeline and my grin went away. Regardless of what she'd done, I couldn't take any pleasure in what was going to happen to her.

I let my mind wander, wish-thinking, wondering if I could be wrong about her ... After all, she had suggested that I go to Myrtle Briscoe and lay my cards on the table. She hadn't insisted on it; but how could she when I, obviously, was as I was: ready to do anything that would keep me out of Sandstone. She could be working with Myrtle. She could be—and her actions with Hardesty didn't prove that she wasn't. She'd have had to lead him on. She couldn't let me beat the truth out of him, perhaps even kill him. She...

Oh, hell. How crazy could a guy get? She'd been working in Doc's dirty racket for years, and it was an easy step from that to—But she might not have known what she was getting into. Doc would have pulled her into it a little at a time, until she was in over her head.

I cursed and sat up. Things didn't happen that way. They never had, so why should they begin now? My whole life had been fouled up. The best I could hope for now was to keep my parole. She was as rotten and crooked as the rest of them, and she'd have to suffer with the rest. But—

I wished I could stop thinking about her.

Almost twenty minutes had passed when Willie tapped on the door and came in with the telephone.

He plugged it into the wall by the bed, and handed it to me. He went out as quietly as he had come in, and I spoke into the mouthpiece. I spoke and listened.

"All right, Doc," I said. "I'll be right over."

I hung up the phone and took a last long look around the room. Then, I got my car out of the garage and drove straight to Madeline's place.

I parked my car behind Doc's and went silently up the stairs. I listened at the door to the bedroom, and then I moved over to the other one.

"It doesn't make sense," Hardesty was saying, angrily. "Our end of the deal was worth twenty-five grand, and we could have wound it up in a couple weeks. I don't see why the hell—"

"All right," Doc's voice cut in. "We make that killing—the last one we could possibly make—and then I do my fade-out. How does that look?"

"The same way it looked in the beginning," said Hardesty. "That's the way we planned it. If you didn't like it, why didn't you say something then?"

"Things have changed since then," said Doc. "The police are looking for Pat or will be shortly. We had to wind up the deal tonight."

"But you intended to wind it up tonight before they ever started looking for Cosgrove," said Hardesty. "Why didn't you tell Madeline and me?"

"I had reasons."

"Oh, hell," said Hardesty, disgustedly.

"I don't get you," said Doc, slowly. "I'd have had two or three weeks' overhead to pay; that's not peanuts. I'd have had to pay several grand in past due bills that I've been stalling. All that would have had to come out of our end. You wouldn't have had more than five or six g's for your cut. What's five or six grand to you, especially when you stand to pick up a clear five?"

"I just don't like it," said Hardesty.

"I can see you don't. But I wonder why."

"Forget it," said Hardesty. "Just forget the whole damned thing."

There was silence then. I raised my fist and knocked.

"Pat?" It was Madeline.

"Yes," I said.

"Come in."

I went in and closed the door.

Hardesty and Madeline were seated on the lounge. She was wearing a nightgown under a blue woolly robe, and her hair had been hastily piled up and pinned on top of her head. She looked like a child, suddenly roused out of a deep sleep, and she gave me a child's questioning but trustful smile. I looked away from her to Doc.

He'd changed clothes, and he was taking more articles of clothing from a pile of bags and packages and putting them into a suitcase which stood on a chair in front of him. He smiled at me, narrow eyed, and jerked his head at Madeline.

"I don't believe you two have met formally," he said. "Mr. Cosgrove—Mrs. Luther."

28

Madeline flirted a hand at me. "'Lo, Mr. Cosgrove," she said in a weak voice.

I nodded to her, dropping into a chair. "How do you do, Mrs. Luther," I said.

"Well," said Doc, with a note of reproof. "You don't seem particularly surprised, Pat."

"I'm not," I said. "I'm only surprised that I didn't see it a long time ago."

"Oh?"

"Yes," I said. "You gave me a tip at the outset, that morning I bought my clothes. You'd been having an argument with Hardesty, and you told him to keep away from your wife. You wanted to be sure of what I'd overheard—whether you'd mentioned Madeline by name."

"I remember," said Doc, shooting an unpleasant glance at Hardesty. "I remember very well, now that you mention it."

"Then there was the matter of the baby," I said. "I didn't believe you'd invented the story. I was sure that your wife had had a baby. Well, I'd seen Lila at pretty close range, thanks to you, and I knew she couldn't have had a baby. So ..."

I didn't tell him the rest; that I'd seen the striae—

167

the marks made by giving birth—on Madeline's body. I wanted to talk about murder, to have him and Hardesty talk about it. With Myrtle Briscoe and her boys listening in.

Hardesty let out an impatient snort.

"For God's sake, Doc," he said, "are we going to sit around here talking all night?"

"There's no hurry," said Doc. "Pat's got a right to some answers. He's entitled to know where he stands . . . Pat, I believe you talked to Lila tonight?"

"Yes," I said.

"And she told you the truth; she doesn't have enough sense to do anything else. Do you see the spot I was in? I was desperate for money, and she fell right into my lap, waiting to be used. And when I'd used her I didn't dare get rid of her. I couldn't separate from a woman I was supposed to be madly in love with. I knew she'd talk if she ever got out from under my thumb."

"And do you see the spot I was in, Pat?" said Madeline, quietly.

"As a matter of fact," I said, "I'm not particularly interested."

Doc grinned and then his expression changed, and he shook his head. "Don't think too hard of her. She doesn't deserve it. We all make mistakes, and we all pay for them. You were only eighteen when you robbed a bank. Madeline was only eighteen when she came here to Capital City."

"I know," I said. "She's a very loyal little woman."

"Very, Pat. To herself, as well as me. We've been husband and wife in name only. She's worked for the money I've given her."

"Would that work include murder?"

"Eggleston's, you mean?" He shook his head calmly.

"She had nothing to do with that. He found out about our marriage and demanded money from her, and I went to make the pay-off. She didn't know I was going to kill him. I didn't either. I didn't even know who'd hired him or whether he was working on his own. I didn't have to talk with him very long, however, to realize that he couldn't be trusted. That left me only one thing to do."

I nodded. That took me off the hook for the murder. Now, to wrap up the rest of it.

Doc glanced at the hall door casually, then back at me. And there was that peculiar look in his eyes again: The one I'd seen back at the house, when Lila had left the room.

"There's one thing I don't understand, Doc," I said. "Why didn't you go through with this Fanning Arnholt deal? Why did you set it all up and then blow it to pieces?"

"That's what I'd like to know!" snapped Hardesty. "I'm just lucky that there's nothing that can be pinned on me."

"Well—" Doc hesitated, grinning faintly, "why don't you make a guess, Pat?"

"I can think of a couple of reasons," I said. "One is that you were trying to get a few marks on the credit side of the ledger. After what happened tonight this state's going to be as clean as a whistle."

"Yes?"

"I think that's what you thought you were doing," I said. "What you persuaded yourself you were doing. Actually, I think you had another motive. You'd got all you could. You intended to make sure that nothing would be left for anyone else."

Doc's fingers tightened on the package he was unwrapping. He stared down at it, blindly, and then he went on picking at the string. He didn't say anything.

Hardesty scowled at him angrily.

"Well, by God!" he said. And then he raised his shoulders in a shrug of helplessness. "Pat, I'm sorry but—"

"I'm talking to Doc," I said. "Let's see if I've got things straight. You'd been wanting to break loose for a long time, Doc. You knew that the next election was going to force you to. You needed to make one last big killing, and when you got my letter from Sandstone you saw a way of doing it with Madeline's and Hardesty's help. You insured yourself heavily in Madeline's—your wife's—favor, you got me out. To kill you, ostensibly, after a quarrel. Actually, of course, you won't get killed. It'll be made to look like I killed you and dumped you in the river where no one could find you. But it won't be that way. You'll clear out and go into hiding, and Hardesty will push the insurance claims through for Madeline. And after a year or so, when it's absolutely safe, she'll join you. Is that what you planned?"

"That," said Doc, "is what I'm going to do. Incidentally, Pat—"

"What about Lila?"

"Well, what about her? My wife wouldn't live with me, but she insisted on the protection of insurance. That's the story."

"It looks to me like the insurance companies will claim fraud. No company would knowingly insure a man with such potentially dangerous living arrangements."

"Correct," Doc nodded. "Too bad they didn't look into the matter more closely. As it is, they've accepted my premiums and Madeline's down as the beneficiary. It's a binding contract and they'll have to pay."

"I see," I said. "How much are you going to have to live on the rest of your life? How much insurance have you got?"

"Well"—he hesitated for a second—"I guess there's no reason why I shouldn't tell you. Ten policies for ten thousand each. It'll come to a hundred thousand, double indemnity."

"What's Hardesty's share?"

"Sixty-five thousand, roughly. A third."

I shook my head. I couldn't think of anything to say for a moment. It seemed to me that everything had been said that needed to be, and it was time for Myrtle to—

"By the way, Pat. As I started to mention a moment ago . . ."

"Yes?" I said.

"It was a nice try—but I'm afraid Myrtle isn't going to be with us. I checked on her whereabouts just before our little soiree at the house. She's out of town."

29

I swallowed, and my Adam's apple stuck in my throat. And I think I must have looked as sick as I felt.

Doc grinned sympathetically. "You weren't going to tell me that you tipped off the police? They'd grab you on that Eggleston rap, and before you could get clear of it—"

"No," I said, "I didn't go to the police. I was just going to say that—that—How can you do it, Doc? You're sentencing me to death! Doesn't that bother you?"

"I suppose it should," said Doc. "But, no, it doesn't. Not much, Pat. You'd have died in Sandstone if I hadn't got you out. This way, at least, you have had a little fling."

"That car Lila bought for me doesn't really mean anything?" I said. "I'm going to be allowed to get away?"

"I'm afraid not, Pat. Not finding my body is one thing. Not finding the man who is supposed to have killed me is another. It would be more than would be swallowed comfortably. You'll have to be caught, I'm afraid, somewhere near the spot of our nominally fatal quarrel."

"And you don't see any danger in my being caught?"

"You mean you'll talk?" He smiled faintly, shucking a pair of socks out of a paper bag. "Who's going to believe a fantastic story such as you'll have to tell when all the evidence points to murder?"

"It isn't going to work, Doc," I said.

"Oh, it'll work all right, Pat," he grinned. "It's just improbable enough to seem completely plausible. You're the best evidence of that yourself. You've had the puzzle in front of you for weeks yet you never arrived at the motive for my getting you out of Sandstone."

"That isn't what I meant," I said. "I'm talking about the insurance companies. They're not going to make settlement on those policies."

"They wouldn't, ordinarily," he nodded. "They wouldn't pay a death claim without positive proof of death—a body, in other words. But where the evidence is so clear cut—well ..."

"What makes you so sure of that?" I said.

"Our friend, Hardesty, here." Doc perked his head. "One of our leading legal lights, regardless of what you may think of him on other grounds. Hardesty says they'll have to pay. If he says so, they will."

That was true. Hardesty *would* know. But why, then, had he wanted me to—? Suddenly, it hit me. The last piece of the murderous puzzle fell into place. And I laughed.

I was caught, stuck in the middle no matter what I did. But I couldn't help laughing.

Hardesty re-crossed his legs, shifting nervously on the lounge. His right hand crept into the pocket of his coat and remained there.

"Doc," I said. "You're not very bright, Doc. Not about some things. I've had a feeling all along that you were into something beyond your depth, but I didn't think you were quite this simple."

"No?" He grinned, but a tinge of red was creeping into his cheeks. "Just how simple am I supposed to be, Pat?"

"Simple enough to believe a man who hates you and loves your wife. Simple enough to believe that he'd be content with a third of that two hundred thousand when he and she can take the whole pile. Sure, he knows what the insurance companies will and won't do. But there's a hell of a big difference between what he knows and what he's told you!"

"I—" Doc looked from Hardesty to Madeline and then back to me. "I don't understand ..."

"There's nothing to understand," said Hardesty curtly. "Don't pay any attention to him, Doc. He—"

"Think it over, Doc," I said. "And while you're doing it, Hardesty can make me his offer. I want you to see why you're going to be killed, but you'll have to think fast. I won't be able to play my part in this little drama if the police catch up with me."

Doc stared at me silently, his eyes blinking behind the thick lenses. I nodded to Hardesty.

"All right," I said. "What's it going to be? Do I kill him and get away or do you do it and let me get caught?"

"Pat!" Madeline cried. "Don't—"

But Hardesty's hand had already come out of his pocket. "You do it," he said, and he tossed the snub-nosed automatic to me. "You do it and get away."

I caught the gun, and motioned with it.

"All right," I said. "Stand up. All three of you."

"Pat," said Hardesty. "You—"

"Up," I said, and yanked him to his feet.

I lined the three of them up, and searched them. I shoved Madeline to one side, and looked at Doc and Hardesty.

"Now," I said, "I'm going to call the police."

"Police!" They spoke the word simultaneously.

"I know," I said. "They won't believe me; probably they won't. But I've got to try."

"But what's it going to get you!" Hardesty's face was dead white. "You could get away, Pat! We'll—I'll see that you have plenty of money to—"

"I don't think so," I said. "A man can't get away from himself."

"You're talking in riddles!" snapped Doc. "You've knocked this insurance scheme in the head. I've cleaned up the political mess. Let it go at that, and—"

"Sure," said Hardesty. "Be sensible, Pat. We're all kind of off on the wrong foot here tonight, but it's not too late to straighten things out ... Doc, why don't we shake hands all around, and—"

"Why not?" said Doc heartily, and his hand shot out.

It closed around my wrist. He bore down on it with all his weight; and Hardesty stepped in close, swinging. And I laughed again. It was too easy. It didn't give me an excuse to really get rough—to give them the only punishment they'd probably ever get.

I weaved around a few of Hardesty's windmill swings, letting him wear himself out. Then I gave him an open-palmed uppercut, and he rose up on his toes and shot backwards, and went down in a heap against the wall.

Doc was still struggling with my gun hand. I let it sag suddenly, jerked upward again, and he went back against the wall with Hardesty.

They sprawled there, looking at me dazedly.

I looked at Madeline, and she was smiling at me happily, joyously. Hugging herself. And before I could think, wonder if I had been right, if just this one time something would go right . . . the bedroom door banged open.

Myrtle Briscoe walked in. Myrtle and two state troopers. She blew a whistle and two more troopers burst through the hall door.

She pointed, and the troopers took hold of Hardesty and Doc. She jerked her head and they started toward the hall with them. It happened in split seconds, so fast that Doc and Hardesty lacked even time for surprise. They went out the door, wordlessly, tottering between the troopers, and Myrtle patted Madeline on the shoulder.

"Our girl friend beat you to the tip-off, Red," she grinned. "Had yourself a pretty bad thirty minutes, didn't you?"

"I—uh—yes, ma'am," I said.

"Well, you asked for it. Tried to get you to level with me, didn't she? I tried, didn't I?"

"Yes, ma'am."

"Well—" her eyes swept over me swiftly, "that little tussle doesn't seem to have hurt you any. I was afraid there might be shooting if I busted in on it. Couldn't let you get shot before I got you a pardon."

"No, ma'am—*what?*" I said.

"Why not?" said Myrtle Briscoe. "I think the governor's going to sign just about anything I lay in front of him."

And she clumped out the door, slamming it behind her, and Madeline was in my arms.

30

That, I believe, is about all.

I got my pardon. I got the job, which I still have, as investigator with the Department of Corrections. Madeline got her divorce, and we got married.

Doc got ninety-nine years for Eggleston's murder, plus an additional thirty years—to run consecutively—for bribery and attempted fraud. Hardesty got a total of forty years.

That's a lot of "gots," and there are still more concerning Burkman and Flanders and the rest of Doc's old gang. But I won't go into those. I'll only say that Doc doesn't lack for friends, if they can be called that, there in Sandstone.

Lila ...

Well, Lila did quite well for herself, everything considered.

She sold her life story, ghost-written, of course, to a newspaper syndicate. That got her a nice chunk of money and a great deal of publicity, very valuable as it turned out. The last I saw of her—Madeline and I— she was headed for Hollywood with a B-picture contract.

She stopped to say good-bye to us before she left. Afterwards, I caught Madeline looking at me thoughtfully.

"I'm wondering," she said. "I'm wondering if I ever will know what went on between you and that dame."

"What went on?" I said. "Surely, you don't think I'd ... do *that,* Mrs. Cosgrove!"

"Uh-hah. I'll bet you wouldn't!"

"Well," I said, "I don't know of anything I can say to convince you ..."

"And you can't think of anything to do either?"

"As a matter of fact," I said, "I believe I can. You've given me an idea."

It wasn't a new idea, but it proved to be a very, very good one. Good enough to make Madeline forget all about Lila.

Good enough, period.

About the Author

James Meyers Thompson was born in Anadarko,
Oklahoma, in 1906. He began writing fiction at a very
young age, selling his first story to *True Detective*
when he was only fourteen. In all, Jim Thompson
wrote twenty-nine novels and two screenplays (for
the Stanley Kubrick films *The Killing* and *Paths of
Glory*). Films based on his novels include: *Coup
de Torchon (Pop. 1280)*, *Serie Noire (A Hell of a
Woman)*, *The Getaway*, *The Killer Inside Me*, *The
Grifters*, and *After Dark, My Sweet*. A biography
of Jim Thompson will be published by Knopf.

VINTAGE CRIME / **BLACK LIZARD**

___ **The Far Cry** by Fredric Brown $8.00   0-679-73469-4

___ **His Name Was Death** $8.00   0-679-73468-6
    by Fredric Brown

___ **I Wake Up Screaming** $8.00   0-679-73677-8
    by Steve Fisher

___ **Black Friday** by David Goodis $7.95   0-679-73255-1

___ **The Burglar** by David Goodis $8.00   0-679-73472-4

___ **Cassidy's Girl** $8.00   0-679-73851-7
    by David Goodis

___ **Night Squad** by David Goodis $8.00   0-679-73698-0

___ **Nightfall** by David Goodis $8.00   0-679-73474-0

___ **Shoot the Piano Player** $7.95   0-679-73254-3
    by David Goodis

___ **Street of No Return** $8.00   0-679-73473-2
    by David Goodis

___ **A Rage in Harlem** $8.00   0-679-72040-5
    by Chester Himes

___ **Shattered** by Richard Neely $9.00   0-679-73498-8

___ **After Dark, My Sweet** $7.95   0-679-73247-0
    by Jim Thompson

___ **Cropper's Cabin** $8.00   0-679-73315-9
    by Jim Thompson

___ **The Getaway** $8.95   0-679-73250-0
    by Jim Thompson

___ **The Grifters** $8.95   0-679-73248-9
    by Jim Thompson

___ **A Hell of a Woman** $8.95   0-679-73251-9
   by Jim Thompson

___ **The Killer Inside Me** $9.00   0-679-73397-3
   by Jim Thompson

___ **Nothing More Than Murder** $9.00   0-679-73309-4
   by Jim Thompson

___ **Pop. 1280** by Jim Thompson $8.95   0-679-73249-7

___ **Recoil** by Jim Thompson $8.00   0-679-73308-6

___ **Savage Night** $8.00   0-679-73310-8
   by Jim Thompson

___ **A Swell-Looking Babe** $8.00   0-679-73311-6
   by Jim Thompson

___ **The Burnt Orange Heresy** $7.95   0-679-73252-7
   by Charles Willeford

___ **Cockfighter** $9.00   0-679-73471-6
   by Charles Willeford

___ **Pick-Up** by Charles Willeford $7.95   0-679-73253-5

___ **The Hot Spot** $8.95   0-679-73329-9
   by Charles Williams

THE KILLER INSIDE ME

In a small town in Texas, there is a sheriff's deputy named Lou Ford, a man so dull that he lives in clichés, so good-natured that he doesn't even lay a finger on the drunks who come into his custody. But then, hurting drunks would be too easy. Lou's sickness requires other victims—and will be satisfied with nothing less than murder.

0-679-73397-3/$9.00

NOTHING MORE THAN MURDER

Sometimes a man and a woman love and hate each other in such equal measure that they can neither stay together nor break apart. Some marriages can only end with murder. And some murders only make the ties of love and hatred stronger.

0-679-73309-4/$9.00

POP. 1280

As high sheriff of Potts County, a godless, loveless hellhole in the American South, Nick Corey spends most of his time eating, sleeping, and avoiding trouble. If only people would stop pushing Nick around. Because when Nick is pushed, he begins to kill. Or to make others do his killing for him. The basis for the acclaimed French film noir, *Coup do Torchon*.

0-679-73249-7/$8.95

SAVAGE NIGHT

Is Carl Bigelow a fresh-faced college kid or a poised hit man tracking down his victim? And if Carl is really two people, what about everyone around him?

0-679-73310-8/$8.00

A SWELL-LOOKING BABE

The Manton looks like a respectable hotel. Dusty Rhodes looks like a selfless young man working as bellhop. The woman in 1004 looks like a slumming angel. But sometimes looks can kill—as Jim Thompson demonstrates in this vision of crime novel as gothic.

0-679-73311-6/$8.00

Available at your local bookstore, or call toll-free to order:
1-800-733-3000 (credit cards only). Prices subject to change.

V I N T A G E   C R I M E